Leen Nolwerk

FROZEN ASSETS

P. G. WODEHOUSE

FROZEN ASSETS

UNABRIDGED

PAN BOOKS LTD : LONDON

First published 1964 by Herbert Jenkins Ltd.

This edition published 1969 by Pan Books Ltd.,
33 Tothill Street, London, S.W.1

330 02202 4

Printed and bound in England by
Hazell Watson and Viney Ltd
Aylesbury, Bucks

Contents

CHAPTER ONE

THE Sergeant of Police who sat at his desk in the dingy little Paris police station was calm, stolid and ponderous, giving the impression of being constructed of some form of suet. He was what Roget in his Thesaurus would have called 'not easily stirred or moved mentally', in which respect he differed sharply from the large young man standing facing him, whose deportment resembled rather closely that of a pea on a hot shovel. Jumpy was the word a stylist would have used to describe Jerry Shoesmith at this moment, and a casual observer might have also supposed that he was a prime suspect undergoing the French equivalent of the third degree.

This, however, was not the case. The reason for his agitation was a more prosaic one. He had come on this last night of his Paris holiday to notify the authorities that he had lost the wallet containing the keys to the apartment lent to him for the duration of his visit. And what was exercising him was the problem of where, should the thing remain unfound, he was going to sleep.

So far, though he had been in the Sergeant's presence for more than a minute, he had made no progress in the direction of informing him of his dilemma. The Sergeant, who on his entry had been stamping official documents in the rhythmical manner of a man operating the trap drums, was still stamping official documents, appearing to have no outside interests. It seemed a shame to interrupt him, but Jerry felt it had to be done.

'Excuse me,' he said, or, rather, 'Pardon, monsieur,' for he was speaking the language of France as far as he could manage it.

The Sergeant looked up. If he was surprised to hear a human voice when he had supposed himself to be alone with his stamping, he gave no sign of it. His was a face not equipped to register emotion.

'Sir?'

'It's about my wallet. I've lost my wallet.'

'Next door. Office of the Commissaire's secretary.'

'But I've just been there, and he told me to come here.'

'Quite in order. You notify him, and then you notify me.'

'So if I notify him again, he will notify me to notify you?'

'Precisely.'

'You mean I go to him—?'

'Just so.'

'And he sends me to you?'

'Exactly.'

'And then you send me to him?'

'It is the official procedure in the case of lost property.'

Jerry gulped, and what the Sergeant would have called a *frisson*, not that he ever had them himself, passed through him. His spirits sank to an even lower low. He perceived that he was up against French red tape, compared to which that of Great Britain and America is only pinkish. Where in the matter of rules and regulations London and New York merely scratch the surface, these Gauls plumb the depths. It is estimated that a French minor official, with his heart really in his work, can turn more hairs grey and have more clients tearing those hairs than any six of his opposite numbers on the pay rolls of other nations.

'Strike me pink,' he said, awed. 'It's like playing Here We Go Round The Mulberry Bush.'

The Sergeant said he had never played Here We Go Round The Mulberry Bush.

'You should,' Jerry assured him. 'You'd be good at it. You might become amateur champion, though you would have stiff competition from the Commissaire's secretary. What happens after you've sent me to him? Does he send me to Brigitte Bardot?'

The Sergeant explained – patiently, for he was a patient man – that Mademoiselle Bardot had no connection with police work. Jerry thanked him.

'Well, anyway,' he said, 'now that I have your ear for a moment, may I repeat that I have lost my wallet. It had my money and my keys in it. Fortunately I was carrying my passport and return ticket in the breast pocket of my coat, or I should have lost those, too. And I've got to be back in London tomorrow.'

'You are English?'

'I am.'

'You speak French not so badly.'

'I picked it up here and there. I read a lot of French.'

'I see. Your accent leaves much to be desired, but you make yourself understood. Proceed, if you please. Tell me of this wallet.'

'Well, it's a sort of combination wallet and key case. It has compartments for money on one side and clips to attach keys to on the other. Very convenient. Unless, of course, you lose the damn thing.'

'If you lose it, you lose everything.'

'You do.'

'Puts you in an awkward position.'

'You never spoke a truer word. That is exactly what it puts you in.'

The Sergeant stamped some more papers, but absently, as if his thoughts were elsewhere.

'Where,' he asked, 'did you lose this wallet? That is the first thing to ascertain. When you say you have lost some object, you must mean that at a certain time, in a certain place, you had it and that at another time and in another place you did not have it. When do you remember having it, and when do you remember—'

'Not having it?'

'Precisely.'

Jerry reflected.

'Well, I must have had it at the cinema, because I took it out to pay for my ticket. I may have dropped it there.'

'Which cinema?'

'The one down the street.'

For the first time the Sergeant showed a certain mild animation.

'I know the cinema you mean. When off duty, I sometimes go to it myself. I went last week. What's showing there now?'

'I can't remember the name of the film, but Caroline Jasmine was in it. It was about a little flower-girl who becomes a great movie star because she has such a fascinating look in her eyes. Then one day it's discovered that one of her eyes is glass, and her career is ruined.'

'Ah, then they've changed the bill. The one I saw was about a girl, very poor and innocent, who meets a man, very rich and dissolute. He falls in love with her, and she gives herself to him in the hope of reforming him. But associating with him turns her into a trollop, while he, transformed by her original purity, repents and goes into a monastery. Made me laugh, that did. Quite a mix-up.'

Jerry agreed that a certain amount of confusion had resulted, but his one-track mind returned to the point at issue. Nothing could be more delightful than this exchange of views on the Arts with one who was plainly a sound critic, but business was business. Interrupting the other as he began to stamp again, he brought the conversation back to the subject of his bereavement.

'About my wallet.'

'Ah, yes.'

'We were talking about my having lost it, if you remember.'

'I had not forgotten. What was it made of, this wallet?'

'Leather.'

'What kind of leather?'

'Crocodile.'

'What colour?'

'Maroon.'

'How big?'

'About six inches long.'

'Had it initials?'

'G.S. in gold letters.'

The Sergeant recalled now that a wallet of precisely this description, discovered on the floor of the cinema down the street, had been brought to him less than a quarter of an hour ago, but he was a self-respecting French official and was not going to allow a thing like that to interfere with the leisurely rhythm of procedure. He resumed his investigations.

'This wallet of which you speak. It contained your keys?'

Jerry reminded him that that was the whole point of these proceedings, and the Sergeant nodded understandingly.

'How many keys?'

'Two.'

'To what?'

'I beg your pardon?'

'Of what doors were they the keys?'

'Oh, I see what you mean. The outer and inner doors of my apartment.'

'You own an apartment in Paris?'

'I'm sorry. I used the word "my" loosely. It was lent me by my uncle. He keeps this apartment and runs over for week ends.'

The Sergeant so far forgot himself as to whistle.

'Must be rich.'

'He is. He's a solicitor, and these legal sharks always have plenty.'

'And he lent the apartment to you?'

'Yes. When I told him I was coming to Paris, he told me I could use it and save hotel bills. I thought it a most admirable arrangement ... till tonight, when I found I couldn't get into the damned place.'

'Because you had lost your keys?'

'Yes, that was the reason. You mustn't think there was any reluctance on my part to get in, because there wasn't. I was all for it.'

The Sergeant stamped some more papers. He had a wristy follow-through which at any other moment Jerry would have admired.

'What size were these keys?'

'One was big, one was small.'

'One big, one small.' The Sergeant pursed his lips. 'That's a bit vague, isn't it? Could you describe them?'

'The little one was flat, and the big one was round.'

'Round?'

'Well, sort of round. Like any other key.'

'Like any other key . . . That's not much help, is it? Was the key-bit of the smaller key grooved?'

'I beg your pardon?'

'I asked you, was the key-bit of the smaller key grooved? That's clear enough, isn't it?'

'No.'

'It is not grooved?'

'I don't know.'

The Sergeant raised his eyebrows.

'Really, sir! I asked you was it grooved, and you said no. Now you say you don't know. We shall not get much further at this rate.'

'I didn't mean No, it's not grooved. I meant No, it wasn't clear enough.'

'I could scarcely have made it clearer,' said the Sergeant stiffly. 'A key-bit is either grooved or it is not grooved.'

'But I don't know what a key-bit is.'

The Sergeant drew his breath in sharply. He seemed incredulous.

'You don't know what a key-bit is?' He took a bunch of keys from his pocket. 'Look, see? That's the key-bit, the part of the key which you insert in the keyhole. Now can you tell me if yours is grooved?'

'No.'

As far as his features would allow him to, the Sergeant registered satisfaction.

'Aha!' he said. 'Now we are getting somewhere. It is *not* grooved?'

'I don't know. You asked me if I could tell you if my key-bit is grooved, and I'm telling you that I can't tell you. For all I know, it may have been grooved from birth. Look here,' said Jerry desperately, 'is all this necessary?'

The Sergeant frowned. He was an equable man, but he could not help feeling that his visitor was being a little difficult.

'These things have to be done in an orderly manner. We must have system. But if you wish, we will leave the matter of the keys for the moment. Now about the money. How much was there in the wallet?'

'Not much.'

'You could not be more exact?'

'I remember there was a mille note and some odd change, call it two hundred francs.'

'So we'll say twelve hundred francs and two keys, one large, the other smaller, the latter with its key-bit possibly grooved, possibly not. Does that satisfy you as a description of the contents?'

'Yes.'

'And the wallet was made of leather?'

'Yes.'

'Crocodile leather?'

'Yes.'

'Maroon in colour?'

'Yes.'

'In length six inches?'

'Yes.'

'With the initials G.S. in gold letters?'

'Yes.'

'I have it here,' said the Sergeant, opening a drawer. 'I was thinking all along that this might be it. The key-bit *is* grooved,' he went on, cutting short Jerry's cry of rapture. He emptied the wallet of its contents, and counted the money. 'Twelve hundred and twenty francs, not twelve hundred as stated.' He measured the wallet with a ruler, and shook his head. 'It's not six inches in length, it's five and a half. Still, I'm not the man to be finnicky. I'll draw up a report for you to sign,' he said, taking three sheets of paper, interleaving them between carbons and starting to write with great care, rather like an obese child working at its copybook. 'Your name?'

'Gerald Shoesmith.'

'Gerald ... that is your surname?'

'No, my christian name.'

'In that case you should say Zoosmeet, Gerald.'

'Can't I have my wallet and go? I want to get to bed.'

'All in good time, sir. Your home address?'

'Three Halsey Chambers, Halsey Court, London.'

'H-a-l-l-s-e-a?'

'H-a-l-s-e-y.'

'Two letters wrong, deleted and initialled. Your age?'

'Twenty-seven.'

'Your profession?'

'Journalist. Newspaper man. Well, actually, at the moment, I'm editor of a paper called *Society Spice*.'

'Connected with the Press, shall we say?' The Sergeant continued to write, murmuring to himself the while. Jerry caught the words '... who was unable to specify if his key-bit was grooved.' He finished and read the statement through, slowly and carefully as one might read a Dead Sea Scroll. 'Yes, that seems to be in order, so ... Please!' he exclaimed as Jerry, having signed the document, reached eagerly for the wallet. 'Not so fast. Access to the property is not permitted until everything is in order.'

'But I understood you to say that everything was in order.'

'Except for the stamps, to be attached to the written and signed statement.'

'How much are you charging for those?'

'Twenty francs.'

'There they are, right in front of you.'

'But they are part of the contents of the wallet.'

'Well, take them out.'

The Sergeant looked shocked. Probably no such breach of the regulations had ever been suggested to him.

'Remove twenty francs from the wallet?' he whispered hoarsely.

'Why not?'

'Impossible. Suppose you made a complaint that the sum was missing when the property was returned to you?'

'I wouldn't dream of doing such a thing.'

'I have no means of knowing that. We must be orderly.'

'And leisurely.'

'Sir?'

'Nothing. I was just thinking it's nice to feel we're not in any hurry.'

'I shall be here all night.'

'So shall I, apparently.' A long, shuddering groan escaped Jerry. 'I wonder,' he said, 'if you would mind if I buried my face in my hands for a moment? There is nothing, I hope, in the regulations to prohibit the poor devils who call at your office from burying their faces in their hands? I shall probably want to cry a little, too, if that's not forbidden. I will be with you again in a minute.'

The interval before he looked up was only slightly longer than that. When he did so, it was in a more cheerful spirit.

'I know what,' he said. 'It's just occurred to me. Lend me twenty francs.'

'Out of my own pocket?' cried the Sergeant, aghast.

'You'll get it back with interest – substantial interest, I may say. I'll write you a receipt for two hundred francs, and you can take that out of the wallet. As a matter of fact, I'd be quite willing to make it a mille . . .'

His voice died away. The Sergeant's look had become stony.

'So you're trying to bribe me, are you?'

'No, no, of course not. Just showing my gratitude to you for doing me a service.'

'When I'm on duty,' said the Sergeant austerely, 'I don't do services. I'm in the service of the law.'

'And what a law! Made by contented half-wits.'

'What!'

'You heard.'

'Yes, sir, I did hear, and if you aren't careful, I'll arrest you for insulting behaviour.'

'I'm not insulting you. I didn't say you were a half-wit,' said Jerry, with the feeling that if he had done so, he would have been guilty of the most fulsome flattery. 'It's the law I'm beefing about. You didn't make the law.'

'But I administer it.'

'I'll say you do. In spades.'

'Your manner borders on the offensive, sir. I've half a mind to arrest you for vagrancy.'

'Who's a vagrant? I'm not.'

'You have no money on your person.'

'No, because you've got it. I think,' said Jerry, 'with your kind permission I will bury my face in my hands again.'

Silence fell once more, a wounded silence on both sides of the desk. Pique was rife, as was dudgeon, and the Entente Cordiale found itself at its lowest ebb. The Sergeant began stamping papers again in a marked manner, and Jerry, raising his head, lit a sullen cigarette. Then suddenly he uttered a cry which caused the Sergeant to hit his thumb instead of the document.

'I've got it! Why didn't we think of that before? Look. Follow me closely here, because I believe I've found a formula acceptable to all parties. You require twenty francs for the stamps. Correct? There are twelve hundred and twenty francs in the wallet. Agreed? Well, then, here's what you do. Change the statement, making the amount of money in that blasted wallet twelve hundred, extract twenty francs, deposit them in the national treasury, and everybody's happy. How's that for constructive thinking?'

The Sergeant sucked his thumb, which seemed to be paining him. The umbrage he had taken had subsided, but he was plainly dubious.

'Change the statement? But it is already written, initialled and signed.'

'Write a new one.'

'I have used up all my carbon paper.'

'Get some more.'

'But would what you suggest be in order?'

'Take a chance. Remember what the fellow said – *De l'audace, et encore de l'audace, et toujours de l'audace.*'

For some moments the Sergeant continued to waver. Then he rose.

'I'll have to cover myself first. I couldn't do anything like that without official sanction. Excuse me,' he said, and passed ponderously through the door that led to the office of the Secretary of the Commissaire.

The Secretary was a fussy little man with glasses and a drooping moustache. He looked up irritably as the door opened, his petulance caused, no doubt, by resentment at being interrupted while talking to a girl as pretty as the one seated before his desk. She had come in a moment ago, a small, trim, alert girl whose tiptilted nose, bright hazel eyes and brisk manner had made an immediate appeal to him.

They made an immediate appeal to the Sergeant also, and the thought passed through what may loosely be called his mind that some people have all the luck. Here was the Secretary enjoying a cosy chat with a delightful member of the other sex, while all he, the Sergeant, drew was jumpy young men who spoke disrespectfully of the laws of France and were unsound, if not definitely shaky, on key-bits. But remembering that he was here on official business, he fought down his self-pity.

'I am sorry to trouble you,' he said, 'but in the absence of the Commissaire I would like your ruling on an important point that has come up. The gentleman you sent to me just now, the one who had lost his wallet.'

'Ah yes, the English newspaper man Gerald Zoosmeet.'

'Zoosmeet, Gerald,' said the Sergeant, scoring a point.

The girl, who had been attending to her face, lowered the lipstick, interested.

'Zoosmeet? Did I hear you say Zoosmeet?'

'Yes, mademoiselle.'

'It can't be. There isn't such a name.'

'Pardon me, mademoiselle, I have it written down here. The gentleman gave it to me in person. He spelled it for me.'

The girl looked at the paper he held out to her, and squeaked excitedly.

'Oh, *Shoesmith*.'

'Precisely, mademoiselle. As I said.'

'And Gerald at that. Well, I'll be darned. I know a Jerry

Shoesmith. Is this one large? Solid bone structure? Lots of firm flesh?'

'Yes, mademoiselle, he is substantial.'

'Reddish hair? Greenish eyes?'

'Yes, mademoiselle.'

'And rather a lamb?'

The Sergeant weighed this, as if not sure that he was justified in bestowing the honourable title of lamb on one who spoke subversively of the law and knew practically nothing about key-bits. However, he stretched a point.

'The gentleman is careless in his speech and apt to become excitable, but otherwise he appears to be of a sufficiently amiable disposition.'

'And you say he's a newspaper man. It must be the same. I met him on the boat coming over from New York two years ago. It turned out that he was a great friend of my brother, so of course we fraternized. He was feeling a bit sorry for himself at the time, because he had been a New York correspondent of one of the papers and they had fired him. Did he say what he was doing now?'

'He describes himself as an editor.'

'I wonder what he's editing. Probably one of those intellectual weeklies. You wouldn't think it to talk to him, but one or two little things he let fall when we were on the boat gave me the idea that at heart he was an egghead.'

'Indeed, mademoiselle?'

'Interested in literature and the arts and all that sort of thing. He told me he had contributed to the *New Statesman* and the *Thursday Review*, and you can't do that unless your head's fairly eggy.'

'No doubt, mademoiselle.'

'But don't get me wrong. When I say he's an egghead, I don't mean a sniffy, superior egghead. He's one of the boys all right. If he wasn't, he wouldn't be a friend of my brother's, because my brother's standards are very exacting. I simply mean that under a blithe exterior he conceals hidden depths.'

'Precisely, mademoiselle. That is often the way.'

The Secretary intervened, speaking rather frostily. He was

18

feeling that this get-together was becoming too chatty, too much like an old-world *salon*, and that there was far too great a tendency on the part of the speakers to leave him out of the conversation.

'You were about to ask my advice, Sergeant,' he said, and the Sergeant got the message. He did not blush, for his cheeks were already ruddier than the cherry, but he quivered a little like a suet pudding in a high wind.

'Yes, sir. A problem has arisen. Do you think that in the case of the loss of an object containing money the cost of the receipt stamps for the written statement of the loss could be met from the contents of the object itself?'

'Mr Zoosmeet has no money in his possession?'

'None, sir. The object – a wallet (one), crocodile leather, colour maroon, five and a half inches in length – contains all his assets.'

'In that case, certainly.'

'Can I change the sum in the written statement so as to avoid any possible future recriminations?'

'I see no objection.'

'And can you lend me two sheets of carbon paper?'

'With pleasure.'

'Thank you.'

'Hey, Sarge,' said the girl, calling after him as he started for the door, 'try to keep Zoosmeet there till I'm through with this gentleman. I want a word with him.'

'I will endeavour to do so, mademoiselle.'

The Sergeant lumbered off, and the Secretary turned to his visitor.

'Now, mademoiselle, what can I do for you? Would you, by the way, prefer that we conducted our conversation in English? I speak English fluently.'

'It would be a convenience. After two years in Paris I can talk French fairly well, but it always makes my nose tickle. Do you find that when you're talking English?'

'No, mademoiselle, I have not had that experience. But perhaps you would be good enough to state your business. Have you, like your friend Mr Zoosmeet, sustained a loss?'

'Yes, I've—'

'One moment, if you please. We must do these things in an orderly manner. Might I have your name?'

'Kay Christopher.'

'Christopher, K. The K. stands for?'

'Well, I suppose, if you delved into it, you'd find it was short for Katherine, but I've always been called Kay. K-a-y. It's quite a usual name in America.'

'You are American?'

'Yes.'

'You have some form of employment in Paris?'

'I work on the *New York Herald-Tribune*.'

'A most respectable paper. I read it myself to improve my English. And what have you lost?'

'My brother.'

The Secretary blinked. He had been thinking more in terms of miniature poodles.

'He's been missing for two days. He and I share an apartment, and two days ago I noticed that he was not among those present, so after waiting awhile and not hearing a word from him I thought I'd better come along to the police.'

'Have you made enquiries at the hospitals?'

'Every one of them. They haven't seen him.'

The Secretary was just about to mention the Morgue, but changed his mind.

'Two days, you say?'

'Nearly that. I leave for work early and he sleeps late, so he may have been in his room when I pulled out the day before yesterday, but he certainly wasn't there that night and he wasn't around next morning. That's when I felt I ought to take steps of some kind. I'm not really panic-stricken, mind you, because he's been away from the nest before and always returned, but ... well, you know how it is, one gets a little anxious when it comes to two days and not a yip out of him.'

'Quite understandable. Anxiety is inevitable. Well, I can assure you that the police will do all that is within their power. What is your brother's name?'

'Edmund Biffen Christopher. Sorry. Christopher, Edmund Biffen.'

'Bee-fawn. An odd name. I do not think I have heard it before.'

'He was called that after a godfather.'

'I see.'

'And strangely enough it's not the Biffen he objects to so much as the Edmund. He says Edmund always makes him think of a fat, pompous old bore with false teeth and a double chin.'

'Indeed?' said the Secretary, wincing a little. His own name was Edmond, and until now he had always thought rather highly of it.

'Fortunately everyone calls him Biff.'

'I see. And what is his age?'

'Twenty-nine. Thirty in a week or so. Old enough to start behaving himself, wouldn't you say?'

'And his profession?'

'He used to be a reporter in New York until one day he suddenly decided to come to Paris. He's writing a novel, only he hasn't got far with it. He doesn't seem able to satisfy his artistic self. He keeps clutching his brow and muttering "This damned thing needs dirtying up." You know how it is when you're writing a novel these days. If it isn't the sort of stuff small boys scribble on fences, nobody will look at it.'

'Shall we say Profession, novelist?'

'If you don't mind stretching the facts a little.'

'Could you now give me some idea of his personal appearance?'

Kay laughed. She had a very musical laugh, the Secretary thought.

'Oh, sure,' she said. 'That's easy. He looks like a dachshund.'

'Pardon?'

'Well, he does. Sharp, pointed features. Animated manner, brown eyes, brown hair, brown suit, brown shoes. Longish nose and not much chin. Just like a dachshund.'

'I see. And his frame of mind. Has he been in good spirits?'

'Excellent.'

'Any financial worries?'

'At the moment, rather fewer than usual, as a matter of fact. That godfather I spoke of died recently in New York, leaving millions, and Biff has an idea he may be in line for a small legacy. He says it's the least the man could do after getting him christened Edmund.'

The Secretary coughed.

'You feel, then,' he said delicately, 'that we can rule out suicide as a possibility?'

'Good heavens, yes. Biff wouldn't kill himself with a ten-foot pole. Not so long as there was a blonde left in the world.'

'He is fond of blondes?'

'They're his life work. The fear that haunts me is that he may have gone off and married one. I wouldn't put it past him. Still, one must hope for the best.'

'Precisely, mademoiselle. It is the only way. Well, I do not think there are any further questions that I need to ask. Will you please go now and repeat to the Sergeant what you have been telling me.'

'Must I? Couldn't we keep it just between us two?'

'It is the official procedure. No, not through that door. That is reserved for the Commissaire, the Sergeant and myself. You go out and enter through the door leading from the street.'

3

The Sergeant came back to Jerry. His air was that of a diplomat who has solved a problem which has been worrying the Chancelleries for weeks.

'All is in order,' he said. 'I have covered myself.'

'Thank heaven for that,' said Jerry. 'Do you know, I had a feeling you would. There goes a man, I said to myself when you went out, who is going to cover himself.'

'The Commissaire's secretary assures me that there is no

objection to doing what you suggest. There you are,' said the Sergeant some long minutes later as he slowly finished writing, slowly read through what he had written and slowly passed it across the desk. 'Sign, please. Hard, for the carbons. Thank you.'

He stamped the paper, put it on top of the pile already stamped, opened the drawer in which he had placed the wallet, took out the wallet, took twenty francs from it, replaced it in the drawer, locked the drawer.

'Now everything is in order,' he said. 'Here is a copy of your statement. The top copy and one carbon are reserved for the files.'

He seemed to consider the affair closed, and Jerry was obliged to point out that there still remained something to be done.

'But you haven't given me my wallet.'

A faint smile passed over the Sergeant's face. How little, he was feeling, the public knew about official procedure.

'You will call for that in three days' time at the Lost Property Office, 36 Rue Bourdillion,' he said with the genial air of one imparting good news.

Jerry had shot from his seat and was clutching his hair.

'Three *days*! But I'm leaving for England tomorrow!'

'I remember, yes, you told me, did you not?'

'Then where am I going to sleep tonight?'

'Ah,' said the Sergeant, seeming to admit that he had a point there.

He began stamping papers again.

CHAPTER TWO

KAY had decided not to see the Sergeant. The brief glimpse she had had of him in the Secretary's office had left her with the feeling that he was a man from whose conversation little uplift and entertainment were to be derived. She was wrong, of course, for he could have told her some good things about key-bits, but she did not know that. She took up her stand in the street outside his door, hoping that he would cut his interview with Jerry reasonably short.

She had pleasant memories of Jerry and the prospect of meeting him again delighted her. Shipboard friendships are not as a rule durable, but theirs had lingered in her mind with an odd tenacity these last two years. It was with bright anticipation that she awaited the coming reunion.

When at length he appeared, he was tottering a little. His eyes were wild, his limbs twitched and he was breathing heavily. A hart panting for cooling streams when heated in the chase, had one happened to come along at the moment, would have shaken his hand and slapped him on the back, recognizing him immediately as a kindred spirit and a member of its lodge.

Kay hailed him with enthusiasm.

'Hello there, Jerry,' she cried. 'A hearty greeting to you, Zoosmeet.'

He raised a hand in a passionate gesture.

'Are you going in to see the Sergeant?' he said hoarsely. 'Don't do it. That way madness lies.' He broke off, peering at her in the blue light cast from above by the police lantern. '*What* was that you said?' He drew a step closer. 'Good Lord!' he exclaimed, allowing his eyes to bulge in the manner popularized by snails.

Until she had spoken, he had seen in her merely a misty, indistinct female figure hovering on the brink of the fate that is worse than death – viz. being closeted with a police sergeant whose conversational methods reduced even strong men to shells of their former selves, and his only thought had been to save her before it was too late. He was able now to perceive that this was no stranger but an old crony with whom he had walked on boat decks in the moonlight and shuffleboarded on sunny afternoons; with whom, side by side on adjoining deck chairs, he had sat and sipped the eleven o'clock soup. After that session with the Sergeant he had supposed that nothing could ever again make him feel that life contained sunshine and laughter and happiness, but she, by the simple process of popping up out of a trap in the middle of a murky Paris street, had accomplished that miracle. A warm glow, similar to that induced by eleven o'clock soup, permeated his entire system.

This girl had made a profound impression on him in the few short days it had taken the *Mauretania* to cross the Atlantic, and it would have been useless for a cynic to argue that this was merely because they all look good to you at sea. Nor could such a cynic have persuaded him that in his present frame of mind almost anyone who was not the Sergeant would have seemed attractive to him. The thing went deeper than that, far far deeper. Strange feelings were stirring within him, and he had the illusion that cowbells were ringing in his ears.

'Good Lord!' he said. 'You!'

'A word I never like,' said Kay. 'People say it when they're stalling for time, trying to remember your name.'

'You don't think I've forgotten your name!'

'I don't know why you shouldn't have, considering that it's two years since we met and then, after five days on that boat, we never saw each other again. When we parted at Cherbourg, I remember you said we must keep in touch. But you didn't keep in touch.'

'How could I? You were in Paris, and I was tied up with my job in London.'

'I'm glad you got a job all right. You were rather worried on the boat about being one of the unemployed. But you could have written.'

'I didn't know your address.'

'And I didn't know yours.'

'What *is* your address?'

'Sixteen Rue Jacob. Look in some time, why don't you?'

'I've got to be back in London tomorrow.'

'Golly, we are ships that pass in the night, aren't we? When do you expect to be in Paris again?'

'Not for another year.'

'That's too bad. I was hoping we'd see something of each other. Well, how are you after all these long years, Jerry? Fine and dandy?'

'Yes. At least, no.'

'Make up your mind.'

'I'm fine and dandy now, but before I saw you I was feeling extremely blue.'

'And, oddly enough, you're looking extremely blue. I suppose it's that police lamp. Why don't we go somewhere and split a cup of coffee? No sense in standing in this draughty street.'

Jerry sighed. Situated as he was, the cheapest cup was beyond his means.

'There's nothing I'd like better. But I couldn't pay for it.'

'Why, didn't you get your wallet back?'

Jerry laughed bitterly. The old wound was throbbing.

'If you knew the Sergeant, you wouldn't ask that. You don't get things back when he has got hold of them. But how did you know I had lost my wallet?'

'I was chatting with the Secretary next door, and the Sarge blew in and told us all about it.'

'Ah, so you've met the Sergeant. I'm glad of that, because if you hadn't, it might have been difficult to make you understand. He's not easy to explain to the lay mind. Yes, he's got the wallet and refuses to give it up. I don't get it till I call at the Lost Property Office three days from now.'

'That's the French for you. What was in it?'

'All my money and the keys to the apartment where I was staying.'

'Into which you can't get?'

'Into which I can't get.'

'Won't the concierge let you in?'

'There isn't a concierge. It's a maisonette. Very snug, too,

26

if you can get past the front door. This, however, I am un-fortunately unable to do. So coffee's out, I'm afraid.'

'Nonsense. I'll pick up the tab.'

The pride of the Shoesmiths had always been high, and in normal circumstances Jerry would never have permitted a member of the other sex to pay for his refreshment, but this was a special case. After half an hour with the Sergeant he needed fortifying.

'You will?' he said eagerly, the aroma of coffee seeming to play about his nostrils. 'It wouldn't run to a drop of brandy as well, would it?'

'Sure. No stint.'

'I'll reimburse you when I get back to civilization.'

'Don't give it a thought. This is my treat.'

'It's awfully good of you.'

'Not at all. Be my guest.'

2

The bistro they found in the next street was of the humble zinc-counter-and-imitation-marble-tables type and rather fuller than he could have wished of taxi-drivers and men who looked as if they were taking a coffee break after a spell of work in the sewers, but to Jerry it seemed an abode of luxury, what Kubla Khan would have called a stately pleasure dome. As he seated himself in a chair even harder than the one provided for his clients by the Sergeant, a thrill of gratitude to the founder of the feast set him ting-ling.

How few girls, he mused, would have been so hospitable to one who, after all, was a comparative stranger. But then that was what had appealed to him so about Kay Christopher during their ocean crossing – her warmth, her kind-ness, her angelic sympathy. How tenderly she had comforted him when he had told her about his being slung out of that correspondent job. How tactful she had been when a wild shot of his had lost them the shuffleboard semi-finals. And that time when the purser had roped him in to sing at the ship's concert. He had been in a highly nervous state at the prospect, and she had put heart into him. 'It won't be so bad,' she had said, though there she had been mistaken, for his performance had been ghastly even by ship's concert standards.

'Tell me,' he said, when the coffee arrived accompanied by what at first taste seemed to be carbolic acid, but which actually was brandy or something reasonably like it, 'You were saying you had been in conference with the Secretary. What was the trouble? Had you lost something?'

'Odd stuff, this,' said Kay, sipping. 'Probably used for taking stains out of serge suits. Still, it certainly has authority. Lost something, did you say? You bet I had. I've lost Biff.'

Jerry stared.

'Biff? You mean *Biff*? Your brother Biff?'

'There's only one Biff in my life, and if you're going to say that's plenty, I'm with you a hundred per cent. He's disappeared. Vanished into thin air. Gone without a cry and been gone two days.'

'Good heavens! You must be worried.'

'Not particularly. He'll be back when the spirit moves him. He's probably just off on a toot somewhere,' said Kay with sisterly candour, and Jerry, too, felt that this must be the solution of the prodigal's absence. In his New York correspondent days he had seen a great deal of Biff and had come to love him like a brother, but he was not blind to his failings. Irresponsible was the adjective that sprang to the lips when one contemplated Edmund Biffen Christopher. His animation had been a byword in circles where animation was general and his taste for gaiety so pronounced as to cause comment among Manhattan's most uninhibited pleasure seekers.

'Biff was always by way of being the master of the revels.'

'He still is.'

'Living in Paris hasn't changed him?'

'Did you expect it to?'

'He ought to get married.'

'If there exists a wife capable of coping with him. There can't be many of that bulldog breed around. I thought he'd found one a year ago, a girl called Linda Rome. She would

28

have been just right for him – one of those calm, quiet, sensible girls with high standards of behaviour and a will of iron. She would have kept him in order. But she broke off the engagement.'

'Why was that?'

'Because she was so sensible, I suppose. Much as I love Biff I wouldn't recommend him as a husband to any girl who hadn't had experience as a prison wardress and wasn't a trainer of performing fleas on the side. He would drive the ordinary young bride crackers. Linda would have taken him in hand and reformed him, and it's a terrible pity she didn't see her way to going through with it. But let's not talk about Biff, let's take a look at your position. I don't see how one can avoid the conclusion that you're in something of a spot. How are you going to get back to London, if you haven't any money?'

'That part's all right. I have my passport and my return ticket.'

'But you can't get into your apartment and you can't go to a hotel, so where are you going to sleep tonight? Have you given any thought to that?'

'Quite a good deal. I suppose I shall have to camp out in the Bois or on a bench somewhere.'

'Oh, we must try to do better than that. Don't talk for a minute, I want to think.'

She became silent, and Jerry watched her over his cup, not with any real hope, for he knew the problem was insoluble, but because watching her seemed to satisfy some deep need in his spiritual make-up. He would have been content to sit watching her for ever.

'I've got it,' she said.

A wave of emotion poured over Jerry. One of those loud French quarrels had broken out between two of the near-by taxi drivers and the air was vibrant with charges and counter-charges, but he hardly heard them. He was stunned by the discovery that in addition to being the loveliest thing that ever played deck tennis or drank eleven o'clock soup she had a brain that even the deepest thinker might envy. He was conscious of an odd sensation similar to the one experienced by the character in the poem who on honeydew had fed and drunk the milk of Paradise, and he did not need the Heart expert of any of the many London periodicals that went in for Heart experts to tell him what this meant. He was in a position to state without fear of contradiction that here beside him sat the girl he had been searching for all his adult life. There was something about her personality – the way she looked, the way her bright hair curled up at the sides of her little hat, the way she drank coffee and the way the mere sound of her voice got inside one and stirred one up as with a swizzle-stick – that made the thought of leaving her and pining away with the Channel separating them the most nauseating he had ever experienced. He leaned forward impulsively, spilling a good deal of coffee, and was about to put these sentiments into words, to give her what at Tilbury House, where he worked, they called the overall picture, when she spoke.

'I know where you can sleep. At Henry's.'

'Who's Henry?'

'Henry Blake-Somerset. He's in the British Embassy. He'll put you up. It isn't far from here. If you've finished spilling coffee, let's go.'

3

If Henry Blake-Somerset, enjoying a weak whisky and water in his apartment preparatory to going to bed, had been asked by some enquiring reporter what was the last thing he wanted at this late hour, he would almost certainly have specified the intrusion on his privacy of a perfect stranger anxious to be accommodated with lodging for the night. He was tired and ruffled. He had had one of those trying days that come to all minor members of corps diplomatiques from time to time, the sort of day when everything goes wrong and the senior members expend their venom on the junior members, who, having no members junior to themselves to whom to pass the buck, are compelled to suffer in silence. His manner, consequently, when he opened the door to Kay's ring, had nothing in it of the jolly innkeeper of oldfashioned comic opera. He looked more like Macbeth seeing a couple of Banquos.

'Hello, Hank,' said Kay in her brisk way. 'You weren't asleep, were you?'

'I was about to go to bed,' said Henry, and his tone was stiff.

'Just what Jerry here wants to do, and I've brought him along to seek shelter. He's in sore straits. Oh, by the way, Mr Shoesmith, Mr Blake-Somerset.'

'How do you do?' said Jerry effusively.

'How do you do?' said Henry, less effusively.

'Mr Shoesmith, I should mention,' said Kay, 'is passing for the moment under the alias of Zoosmeet, but think none the worse of him for that. It's his only way of getting the secret papers through to the Prime Minister. Where was I? Oh yes, sore straits. Tell him the story of your life, Jerry.'

Jerry embarked on his narrative, but not with any marked ease of manner, for he seemed to detect in his host's eye a certain imperfect sympathy. Henry Blake-Somerset was a small and slender young man of singular but frosty good looks. He had what Jerry had once seen described in a book as enamelled elegance. His hair was light and sleek, his nose aristocratically arched, his lips thin, his eyes a pale and chilly blue. Kay, Jerry recalled, had said that he was attached to the British Embassy, and he could well believe it. Here, obviously, was a rising young diplomat who knew all about protocol and initialling memoranda in triplicate and could put foreign spies in their places with a lifted eyebrow. The thought crossed his mind that if called upon to select a companion for a long walking tour, Henry Blake-Somerset would be his choice only after he had scraped the barrel to its fullest extent. Against this, however, must be set the fact that he had a bed to dispose of, and that made up for everything.

'So you see,' said Kay, as he concluded the story of the lost wallet, 'he's the dove they sent out of the Ark, which could find no resting place, and if you don't do your Boy Scout act of kindness, he'll be in what you Embassy guys call a rapidly deteriorating situation. You can put him in your spare room,' she said, and Henry, with a notable lack of enthusiasm, said Yes, he supposed he could.

'Of course you can,' said Kay. 'There it is, eating its head off. Well, I'll leave you to fix him up. Good night, Hank. Good night, Jerry. If I'm to give my employers of my best tomorrow, I must go and get some sleep.'

Her departure was followed by a longish silence. Jerry was silent because he was thinking of Kay, Henry was silent because he was thinking of Jerry. A young man of regular habits who held strong views on the subject of Englishmen's homes and castles, he resented having perfect strangers thrust on him like stray dogs. Left to himself, he would have finished his whisky and water, wound up his watch, brushed his teeth, gargled a little mouth wash and turned in between the sheets, all set for the refreshing slumber which would enable him to be bright and competent at the Embassy tomorrow. And now this! He did not actually glare at Jerry, but his manner could not have been more distant if the latter had been a heavily veiled woman, diffusing a strange exotic scent, whom he had found helping herself to top secret documents out of the Embassy safe.

However, he was – though unwillingly – a host.

'Can I offer you a drink, Mr Shoesmith?' he said gloomily.

'Thanks,' said Jerry, and instantly regretted the word. This, he realized, would mean conversation, and he was not feeling in the vein for conversation. Love had come to him this night, and he wanted to be alone with his thoughts, not to have to exchange small talk with a man who was making so obvious his distaste for his interior organs. 'I feel awful,' he said apologetically, 'intruding on you like this.'

'Not at all,' said Henry, though with the air of one who would have preferred to say 'And so you damn well ought to.' He took a sip of whisky and water. 'Very glad to be of help,' he said, speaking not perhaps actually from between clenched teeth but certainly the next thing to it.

'I was all set to camp out in the Bois, when Miss Christopher had this sudden inspiration of getting you to put me up.'

'Indeed?' said Henry, his tone indicating only too clearly

what he thought of Kay's sudden inspirations. 'Are you an old friend of hers?'

'Hardly that,' said Jerry, wishing not for the first time that his host's eyes were a little less pale and icy or, alternatively, that if they had to be pale and icy, their proprietor would not direct them at him with such unpleasant intensity, for the young diplomat was making him feel like an unwanted ant at a picnic. 'We were on the same boat coming over from New York two years ago and saw something of each other then. I met her again tonight at the police station.'

'What was she doing there?'

'She had gone to ask the police to find her brother. He seems to have disappeared.'

If it is possible to drink whisky and water with a sneer, Henry did so.

'Probably off on a drinking bout.'

'That was Miss Christopher's theory.'

'The correct one, I imagine. The man's a typical American playboy.'

'I suppose you could call him that. I'm very fond of him myself.'

'You know him?'

'Oh, very well.'

'I understood you to say that you and Miss Christopher were mere acquaintances.'

The expression revolted Jerry, but he supposed that – so far – it more or less fitted the facts.

'We are.'

'Yet you appear to be closely connected with the family.'

'I saw a lot of Biff in New York. He was a reporter on a paper there, and I was the New York correspondent of a London paper. I went around with him all the time.'

'With Miss Christopher also?'

'No, I never met her when I was in New York. I think she was out on the coast. Why do you ask?'

'Oh, no particular reason. I just thought that you and she seemed on excellent terms. I noticed that she called you by your first name.'

'Don't most girls drop the Mister fairly soon nowadays?'

'Do they? I could not say.'

'They do with me. I suppose they find 'Mister Shoesmith' a bit of a tongue-twister. I doubt if you could say it ten times quick.'

Henry Blake-Somerset apparently had no intention of trying. He took an austere sip of whisky and water and was silent for so long that Jerry wondered if he had gone to sleep.

'So you and Miss Chistopher were just shipboard acquaintances,' he said, coming abruptly out of his reverie, and once more Jerry found the description distasteful. 'I thought it possible that you might have been seeing her since.'

'Oh, no.'

'You have not happened to meet her during your stay in Paris?'

'No.'

'The boat trip took how long?'

'Five days.'

'And she calls you by your first name!'

Jerry became a little irritated.

'Well, she calls *you* by your first name.'

'That,' said Henry, rising, 'is no doubt because we are engaged to be married. Will you excuse me now if I turn in. We keep early hours at the Embassy.'

4

His statement that the Embassy staff were expected to clock in at an early hour proved next morning to have been strictly accurate. When Jerry woke, he found himself alone. And he was just sitting down to breakfast, when the telephone rang.

Kay's voice came over the wire.

'Hank?'

'No, he's gone. This is Jerry.'

'Couldn't be better, because you're the one I want to talk to. Have you had breakfast?'

'Just having it.'

'Don't spare the marmalade. It's good. Hank has it imported from Scotland. Listen, what I'm calling up about. I've had a telegram from Biff.'

'You have? Where is he?'

'Over in London, staying at Barribault's Hotel. As if he could afford a place like that, the misguided young cuckoo. Could you find time to go and see him when you get back?'

'Of course.'

'Ask him what he thinks he's playing at, going off without a word. Tell him I've been distracted with anxiety and am under sedatives with an ice pack on my head. Talk to him like a Dutch uncle and grind his face in the dust. Goodbye.'

'Wait. Don't go.'

'I must go. I'm working. Well, I can give you five seconds. What's on your mind?'

Jerry's voice was grim and accusing, the voice of a man who is about to demand an explanation and intends to stand no nonsense.

'You know what's on my mind. Why didn't you tell me you were engaged to this Blake-Somerset disaster?'

'Disaster, did you say?'

'That's what I said.'

'You sound as if you hadn't taken to Hank.'

'I didn't.'

'What's wrong with the poor guy?'

'He's a mess. Totally unfit for human consumption.'

'Well, I'm certainly surprised to hear you talk like that about a man who is your host, with whose food you're at this very moment bursting.'

'I am not bursting. I am making a light Continental breakfast. But that's not the point.'

'What is the point?'

'The point is that you're not going to marry him or any-one else. You're going to marry me.'

There was silence at the other end of the wire. It lasted perhaps a quarter of a minute, though Jerry would have put it at more like a quarter of an hour. Then Kay spoke.

'What did you say?'

'I said you were going to marry me.'

35

'I had an idea that was it, and I suppose you thought I'd fainted. Like Mrs Sanders.'

'Who?'

'Sanders, Mrs, wife of Sanders, Mister. Pickwick Papers. Witness in the case of Bardell versus Pickwick. She told the judge she fainted dead away when Mr Sanders asked her to name the day, and she believed that everybody as called herself a lady would do the same under similar circumstances. Well, I didn't faint, but I must confess to a certain surprise. You're sure you mean me?'

'I love you. I know now that I loved you the first time I saw you. I can't think why I didn't realize it,' said Jerry with the touch of annoyance a man feels when conscious of having carelessly overlooked a matter of some importance. 'I love you, I love you. Well?'

'Well, what?'

'Will you marry me?'

'This is the marmalade speaking, Zoosmeet. It's heady stuff. I ought to have warned you. My good man, you hardly know me.'

'Of course I know you.'

'Five days on an ocean liner.'

'As good as five years ashore. You can't have forgotten those days.'

'I've never forgotten you singing at the ship's concert.'

'Don't make a joke of it. I'm serious.'

'You're crazy.'

'About you. Well?'

'You keep saying "Well?". I suppose you mean you want my views. All right, here they come. You have paid me the greatest compliment a man can pay a woman, or so they all tell me, but I still maintain you're non compos. You simply can't go talking like this to one whose troth is plighted to another. What would Henry say if he heard you? He'd be terribly annoyed and might not ask you to breakfast again. Goodbye,' said Kay, 'I must rush.'

Jerry returned to the breakfast table and took a moody spoonful of marmalade. It was, as Kay had said, extremely good and did credit to the land of its origin, but it accomplished little in the way of raising his spirits. It was a Zoosmeet, Gerald with heart bowed down who finished the dregs of the coffee pot and lit the after-breakfast cigarette. He was thinking of Henry Blake-Somerset, and his thoughts were not agreeable ones. Had he been informed at this moment that Henry, going about his duties at Number 37 Rue Faubourg St Honoré, had tripped over a draft treaty and broken his neck, it is to be feared that his immediate reaction would have been to chant Hosannas like the Cherubim and Seraphim.

CHAPTER THREE

BARRIBAULT'S Hotel, situated in the heart of Mayfair, is probably the best and certainly the most expensive establishment of its kind in London. It caters principally for Indian Maharajas and Texas oil millionaires, plutocrats not given to counting the cost, and as these are men of impatient habit who want what they want when they want it and tend to become peevish if they do not get theirs quick, it sees to it that its room service is prompt and efficient. It was consequently only a few minutes after Edmund Biffen Christopher had placed his order for breakfast on the morning following Jerry's return to London that a waiter wheeled a laden table into his room on the third floor.

This brother of Kay's fully bore out the picture she had sketched for the benefit of the Commissaire's secretary. He not only looked like a dachshund, he looked considerably more like a dachshund than most dachshunds do. Seeing him, one got the feeling that Nature had toyed with the idea of making a dog of this breed and on second thoughts had decided to turn out something with the same sort of face but not so horizontal and with no tail. He greeted the waiter with a 'Hi!' that was virtually a bark, and the waiter said 'Good morning, sir.'

'Your breakfast,' he added rather unnecessarily, for the scent of sausages and bacon was floating over the room like a benediction.

Biff, inspecting the table, saw that Barribault's had given of its abundance. The coffee was there, the bacon was there, the sausages were there, and the eye rested in addition on toast, butter, marmalade, sugar, salt, pepper, cream, mustard and orange juice. A full hand, one might have supposed. Nevertheless, he seemed to feel that there was something missing.

'Isn't there any mail?'

'Sir?'

'I was expecting a cable. It must have come by now.'

'Should I enquire at the desk?'

'Do just that. Christopher's the name.'

The waiter went to the telephone, established communication with the desk and having replaced the receiver came back with the good news he had gleaned from the men up top.

'There is a cable, sir. It is being sent up.'

Biff was unable to click his tongue censoriously, for he had started on the sausages, but he looked annoyed.

'Why didn't they send it up before, blister their insides? I've been in agonies of suspense.'

'Possibly you placed a Do Not Disturb sign on your door, sir.'

Biff was fairminded. He saw the justice of this. Barribault's Hotel had not been negligent and must be dismissed without a stain on its character.

'You're perfectly right, I did. It's a long time since I was in London and I roamed around last night to a rather advanced hour, picking up the threads. You live in London?'

'In the suburbs, sir. Down at Valley Fields.'

'Nice place?'

'Very nice, sir.'

'Got your little bit of garden and all that?'

'Yes, sir.'

'Good for you. I've been in Paris for the last three years. You know Paris at all?'

'No, sir. An agreeable city, I have been told.'

'Well, it's all right in many ways – Springtime on the boulevards and so forth, but everyone talks French there. Sheer affectation, it's always seemed to me. Do you know what you'd be if you were in Paris?'

'No, sir.'

'A garçon, that's what you'd be, and these things would be called saucissons, and where you live would be the banlieu. That just shows you what you'd be up against if you went and settled there. Too silly for words. You know New York?'

'No, sir.'

'You haven't lived. That's the place. Something going on all the time. I was a sap ever to have left it. I had a good job with the *World-Telegram*, knew everybody, went everywhere, had a hundred friends and could rely on getting a hundred laughs daily. Do you know what life was? One grand sweet song, that's what it was, and like a chump I let myself be conned into thinking there was something even better across the Atlantic. All that publicity about Paris and the Left Bank got me hooked, and I came over meaning to write my great novel. You ever written a novel?'

'No, sir.'

'Very sensible. Very testing to the stamina. It's all right when you're rolling back in your chair with a pipe and a little something in a glass, thinking the thing out, but then comes the writing. That's the snag. Very difficult to buckle down to it and get a move on. And talking of getting a move on, how do they deliver mail in this joint? By ox cart? It must be several hours since ... Ah!' He broke off as a knock sounded on the door. 'Entrez,' he shouted. 'Sorry, damn it, I mean Come in.'

A boy entered with an envelope on a salver, was tipped and withdrew. Biff tore open the envelope with fingers that shook a little, scanned its contents with eyes that seemed to protrude like a snail's, and with a gasping cry sank back in his chair, gurgling. The waiter eyed him with concern. Their acquaintanceship had been brief, but like most people who met him he had rapidly come to look on Biff as a familiar friend and his demeanour distressed him. He feared for his well-being. His niece, who lived with him, had recently been presented by her employer with a pedigree Boxer, and only yesterday it had behaved in a similar manner when about to give up its all after a surfeit of ice cream, a delicacy of which it was far too fond.

'Are you ill, sir?' he enquired anxiously, and Biff looked up, surprised.

'Who, me? I should say not. Never felt better in my life.'

'I was afraid you might have had bad news, sir.'

Biff rose and tapped him impressively on his gleaming shirt front. His eyes were glowing with a strange light.

'Waiter,' he said, 'let me tell you something, as you seem interested. I doubt if anyone has ever had better news. I'm floating on a pink cloud over an ocean of bliss while harps and sackbuts do their stuff and a thousand voices give three rousing cheers. Waiter ... But why this formality? May I call you George?'

'It is not my name, sir.'

'What is your name?'

'William, sir.'

'Mind if I address you as Bill?'

'Not at all, sir, though I am usually called Willie.'

A slight frown marred the brightness of Biff's face, like a cloud passing over the sun on a fine summer day.

'This "Sir" stuff, I wish you'd cut it out. It's undemocratic. I don't like it. First names between buddies, don't you think? Well, not exactly first names, because that would mean your calling me Edmund, and you probably feel as I do that there are few fouler labels. Make it Biff, Willie.'

'Very good, sir.'

'Very good *what?*'

'Very good, Biff,' said the waiter with a visible effort.

Biff had risen from his chair and was pacing the room in an emotional manner, his sausages or saucissons temporarily forgotten.

'That's better. Yes, Willie o' man, I was christened Edmund Biffen after a godfather. But don't in your haste start pitying me, because if I hadn't been christened Edmund Biffen, you wouldn't now be chewing the fat with a millionaire. Yes, you heard me. That's what I said, a millionaire. For that's what I am, Willie o' man. This cable tells the story. My godfather, a big wheel named Edmund Biffen Pyke, who recently turned in his dinner pail and went to reside with the morning stars, has left me his entire pile, amounting to more millions than you could shake a stick at in a month of Sundays.'

There was a momentary silence, and then the words 'Cor lumme!' rang through the room. It was unusual for the waiter to use this exclamation, for as a rule he took pains to avoid the vernacular, and the fact that he did so now showed how deeply the news had stirred him. He was a motheaten man in his middle fifties, who looked as if he gardened after hours in his suburban home and on Sundays took around the offertory bag in a suburban church, as was indeed the case. His name was William Albert Pilbeam, and he had a son named Percy, who ran a private enquiry agency, and a niece called Gwendoline, who was secretary to the President of the Mammoth Publishing Company, but this did not show in his appearance. He gaped at Biff, stunned.

'Cor lumme,' he said. 'It's like winning a pool!'

Biff could not have agreed with him more.

'Exactly like winning a pool,' he said, 'because the odds against my bringing home the bacon were so astronomical that I can hardly believe it even now. I can't help feeling there's a catch somewhere. The late Pyke was an austere man and he never approved of me, except once, when I saved him from drowning at his Long Island residence. He didn't like me being pinched by New York's finest for getting into fights in bars, as happened from time to time. He always bailed me out, I'll give him credit for that, but you could see he wasn't pleased. He looked askance, Willie o' man, and when I tried to tell him that boys will be boys and you're only young once, there was nothing in his manner to suggest that I was putting the idea across. Do you often get into fights in bars?'

Mr Pilbeam said that he did not.

'Not even when flushed with wine?'

It appeared that Mr Pilbeam never became flushed with wine. He was, he explained, a total abstainer.

'Good God!' said Biff, shocked. He had known in a vague sort of way that such characters existed, but he had never expected to meet one of them. 'You mean you get by in this disturbed post-war world on lemonade and barley water? You're certainly doing it the hard way. Still, I suppose you avoid certain inconveniences. It gets boring after a while being thrown into the tank, always with that nervous feeling that this time the old man won't come through with the necessary bail. But you know how it is. I like my little drop

of something of an evening, and unfortunately, when I in-
dulge, I seem to lose my calm judgment. That's why I'm in
London. I had to skip out of Paris somewhat hurriedly as
the result of socking an agent de police.'

Mr Pilbeam said 'Good gracious!', adding that strong
wine was a mocker, and Biff said he didn't mind it mocking
him, but he wished it would stop short of leading him on to
swat the constabulary.

'I'd got into an argument with a fellow in a bar and at the
height of the proceedings, just as I was about to strike him
on the mazzard, this *flic* intervened, and his was the mazzard I struck. It was a mistake. I can see that now. But his
manner was brusque and, as I have indicated, I had been
hoisting a few. I managed to escape on winged feet, but I
deemed it best to hop on the next plane to London without
stopping to pack and make my getaway before the authorities started watching the ports. On arriving in London, I
cabled the New York lawyers asking if by any chance there
was some small legacy coming my way, and back comes
this gram informing me that I cop the lot. As you say, very
like winning a pool. The most I was hoping for was a
thousand dollars or so, and I wasn't really expecting that.'
He paused, fixing Mr Pilbeam with a reproachful eye, for
the other was sidling towards the door. 'Are you leaving
me?'

Mr Pilbeam explained that he would greatly have preferred to stay and hear more, for he had been held spell-
bound by even this brief résumé, but duty called him
elsewhere. A waiter's time is not his own.

Biff said he quite understood.

'Heavy day at the office, eh? Then I mustn't keep you.
Would you care to kick me before you go?'

'Sir?'

'It would be something to tell your grandchildren, that
you once kicked a millionaire. No? Well, up to you, of
course. Then I'll just scribble you my autograph,' said Biff.

The door closed. He resumed his breakfast, and never in
the history of sausages and bacon had sausages been so
toothsome, bacon so crisp and palatable. The marmalade,

43

too, had a tang which even Henry Blake-Somerset's imported Dundee could not have rivalled. He was covering the final slice of toast with a liberal smearing of it, when the telephone rang.

'Biff?'

'Speaking.'

'Oh, hullo, Biff. This is Jerry Shoesmith.'

Biff uttered a joyful yelp. Of all his many New York friends, he had always been closest to Jerry.

'Well, fry me for an oyster! What are you doing in London? I thought you were Our Man In America. Aren't you New-York-corresponding any longer?'

'No, I lost that job two years ago. I let the paper in for a libel suit, and they fired me.'

'I'm sorry. That's too bad.'

'My fault. Not that that makes it any better.'

'What are you doing now?'

'I'm editor of one of Tilbury's papers. Don't ask me which one.'

'Of course not. Wouldn't dream of it. Which one?'

'*Society Spice.*'

'My God! But that's a loathsome rag. All glamour girls and scandal, isn't it? Not your cup of tea at all, I'd have thought.'

'It isn't. I hate the foul thing. But I didn't ring you up to talk about my troubles. I want to see you.'

'And I want to see *you*, Jerry o' man. Jerry, the most extraordinary thing has happened. This'll make you whistle. My godfather—'

'Tell me about it later. Can you come to my place at about five?'

'Sure. Where is it?'

'Three Halsey Chambers. In Halsey Court. Just round the corner from Barribault's.'

'I'll be there. Why can't you talk now?'

'I've got to work.'

'Oh, work?' said Biff with a shiver of distaste. It was a nervous habit he himself had always avoided as far as possible.

44

He hung up the receiver and returned to his toast and marmalade.

2

It had been Jerry's intention, when he opened the door of Number Three Halsey Chambers at five o'clock and found Biff on the mat, to start without delay talking to him, as Kay had directed, like one of those Dutch uncles who are so much more formidable than the ordinary run-of-the-mill uncle. In the intervals of assembling next week's *Society Spice* during the afternoon he had thought up several good things to say to him, all calculated to bring the blush of shame to even his hardened cheek, and he was about to give them utterance when Biff raised a restraining hand.

'I know, Jerry o' man, I know. What a long time it is since we saw each other and how well I'm looking and I'm longing to hear all your news and whatever became of old what's-his-name and so on and so forth. But we haven't leisure for all that jazz. Let's take the minutes as read and get down to the agenda. Cast your eye on this,' said Biff, thrusting the cable at him.

Jerry took it, read it with widening eyes, drew a deep breath, stared, read it again and drew another deep breath.

'Good Lord!' he said at length.

'Exactly how I felt.'

'Well, I'll be damned!'

'Just what I said.'

'Who's Pyke, deceased?'

'My godfather.'

'Did he leave much?'

'Millions.'

'And you get it all?'

'Every cent.'

'But that's wonderful.'

'I'm not ill pleased, I must confess.'

'What does it feel like being a millionaire?'

Biff mused for a moment. He had not really analysed his state of mind, but he was able to give a rough idea of it.

45

'It's an odd sensation. Much the same as going up in an express elevator and finding at the half way point that you've left all your insides at the third floor. It's difficult to realize at first that you're one of the higher bracket boys and that from now on money is no object.'

'I can imagine.'

'When you do realize it, you feel a sort of yeasty bene-volence towards the whole human race rather like what you get on New Year's Eve after the second bottle. You yearn to be a do-gooder. You think of all the poor slobs who aren't millionaires and your heart bleeds for them. You want to start fixing them up with purses of gold – bringing the sun-shine into their drab lives, if you get what I mean.'

'I get it.'

'Take you, for instance. Here you are, working on a rag of a paper no right-thinking man would care to be found dead in a ditch with, and nothing to look forward to except a miserable impecunious old age ending in death in a gutter.'

'That's what you read in the tea leaves, is it?'

'That's what. Death in a gutter,' said Biff firmly. 'And why? Because you're short of capital. You can't get any-where in the world today without capital. I've noticed the same thing about myself. I've always been full of schemes, but I never had the cash to promote them. Till now, of course. What you need is a purse of gold, Jerry o' man. I'm pencilling you in for ten thousand pounds.'

'What!'

'Siip of the tongue. I meant twenty.'

'Are you offering me twenty thousand pounds?'

'As a starter. More where it came from, if you need it. Just say the word. After all, we're buddies, you can't get away from that.'

Jerry shook his head.

'No, thanks, Biff. It's awfully good of you, but you'll have to bring the sunshine into somebody else's drab life. I want to be unique.'

'How do you mean, unique?'

'I want to be the only member of your circle who doesn't

46

come trotting up to you and offering to sit in your lap and share the wealth. How many friends have you, would you say?'

'Quite a number.'

'Well, you can take it from me, they'll all try to get their cut.'

'Except you?'

'Except me.'

'Very disappointing,' said Biff, and there was silence for a moment while he seemed to brood on Jerry's eccentric attitude. He himself had never found money anything of a problem. If you had it, fine, you lent it to your pals. If you hadn't, you touched the pals. As simple as that. 'You're sure I can't persuade you?'

'Quite sure.'

'Nothing doing?'

'Nothing.'

'Twenty thousand isn't much.'

'It sounds a lot to me. I'll tell you what I will do, Biff, as you're an old friend. When I've died in my gutter, you can pay the funeral expenses.'

'Right. That's a gentleman's agreement. But it's going to be hard to get rid of all that money if everyone's as unco-operative as you.'

'They won't be,' Jerry assured him. 'They'll be lining up in a queue with outstretched hands like the staff of a Paris hotel when a guest's leaving. When do you collect?'

'Ah, there you have me. They don't say in the cable. They simply say ... but you've read it. And here's something I'd like to have your views on, Jerry. Did you notice something sinister in that cable? The bit at the end?'

'You mean about you inheriting the money in accordance with the provisions of the Trust? Yes, I saw that. I wonder what it means.'

'So do I. What Trust? Which Trust? I don't like the sound of it. They say "Letter follows", so I imagine the explanation will be in that, but it makes me uneasy. Suppose it's one of those freak wills with a clause in the small print saying I've got to dye my hair purple or roll a peanut along Piccadilly with my nose?'

'Was Pyke, deceased, the sort of man to make a freak will?'

'He never gave me that impression. As I was saying to a capital fellow I met at the hotel this morning, he was very much on the austere side. Limey by birth, but converted in the course of the years into the typical American tycoon, all cold grey eye and jutting jaw. Nothing frivolous about Edmund Biffen Pyke when I knew him. But that was three years ago, and I did hear somebody say he'd become a bit on the eccentric side since he retired from business. These big financiers often do, they tell me, when they stop going to the office. They've nothing to occupy their time, and the next thing you know they're going about in a cocked hat with a hand tucked into their waistcoat, saying they're Napoleon. Or cutting out paper dolls or claiming that Queen Elizabeth wrote Shakespeare's plays.'

'Was he very fond of you?'

'If he was, he didn't show it. You remember how, when we were in New York, I was occasionally pinched by the police. Well, on those occasions he gave me the devil. It was like a minor prophet of the Old Testament rebuking the sins of the people. He used to say he'd cure me of that sort of thing if it was the last thing he did. It was quite an obsession with him.'

'Very strange.'

'Very.'

'Well, let's hope you'll be all right.'

'Oh, I shall be all right, whatever happens, because if I have to push peanuts with my nose, I'll do it blithely. I don't intend to let a little thing like that stand between me and a bank roll.'

'That's the spirit. I wouldn't worry about this Trust business. It probably merely means that you don't get the capital cash down but simply collect the interest till you're forty or fifty or whatever it is.'

'Which, as even four per cent on the Pyke millions should work out at around two hundred thousand a year, will be perfectly agreeable to me. I can scrape along on two hundred thousand. The only trouble is that in these legal matters there's always a long stage wait before the balloon goes up. It may be months before I get a cent, and in the meantime funds are running very short. It's not cheap living at Barribault's.'

'What on earth made you go there?'

'Oh, I thought I would. I'm sorry I did, though, now, because, as I say, my sojourn has made the privy purse look as if it had been going in for one of those diet systems. But all is not lost. I've a picture over in Paris that I won in a raffle and was saving for a rainy day. Do you know anything about pictures?'

'Not a thing.'

'Well, this one's a Boudin, and it's quite valuable. I'm going to phone Kay – my sister – did I ever mention her to you? – we share an apartment – to send it to me, and then I'll sell it and be on a sound financial basis again.'

'And while you're waiting to sell it, why don't you move in here with me?'

'May I really?'

'If you can stand the squalor.'

Halsey Court, though situated in Mayfair, was no luxury spot. It was a dark little cul-de-sac in which cats roamed and banana skins and old newspapers collected on the sidewalks, and the flats in Halsey Chambers were in keeping with the general seediness of the locality. Tilbury House did not believe in paying its minor editors large salaries, and the dinginess of the room in which they were sitting testified to the slenderness of Jerry's means. But Biff had no fault to find with it.

'What squalor?' he said. 'I call it snug. You should see my place in Paris after a Saturday night party. Thanks, Jerry, I'll be with you before yonder sun has set. Very handsome of you.'

'A pleasure.'

'I'll check out of Barribault's this evening. By the way,' said Biff, suddenly remembering a point which had been puzzling him since breakfast time, 'there's a mystery you can clear up, if you will be so good. You phoned me at Barribault's this morning. Correct? Well, how on earth did you know I was there?'

'Kay told me.'

Biff stared. He could make nothing of this.

'Pull yourself together, Jerry o' man, and if you're just trying to be funny, don't. She can't have told you. She's in Paris.'

'So was I in Paris. I got back yesterday.'

'Well, I'll be darned. But here's another point. How did you meet Kay? And how did you know it *was* Kay when you did meet her? You had never seen her in your life.'

'Yes, I had. We travelled over on the same boat from New York two years ago. We met the night before last at a police station.'

This interested Biff, himself an old patron of police stations.

'Got herself jugged, did she? Cops finally closed in on her, eh?'

His words revolted Jerry. Like many another young man in love, he found a brother's attitude towards the loved one jarring.

'Not at all. I was notifying the police that I had lost my wallet, and she was notifying them that she had lost you. She was very worried about you, terribly worried.'

No Dutch uncle could have spoken with more reproach, but Biff stoutly declined to show remorse.

'She was, was she? Well, I'm terribly worried about her. I don't suppose she told you, but that child is sticking out her foolish little neck ... what's the matter?'

'Nothing,' said Jerry. He had merely shuddered at hearing Kay's neck so described.

'She's gone and got engaged to a pill of the first water, who can't possibly make her happy. A ghastly Limey ... Sorry, I forgot you were one.'

'Don't apologize. Somebody has to be. A ghastly Limey, you were saying.'

'Fellow in the British Embassy called Blake-Somerset, you wouldn't know him.'

'On the contrary. I not only know him, but have slept in his spare bed and eaten his bread and marmalade. I couldn't get into my apartment, so Kay made him put me up for the night. He didn't seem too pleased.'

'He wouldn't be. Did you gather the impression that he was a pill?'

'Almost immediately.'

'It beats me what she sees in him.'

'I wondered that, too.'

'Well, there it is. Girls are odd. Linda used to perplex me greatly at times. Have you ever met Tilbury's niece, Linda Rome?'

'No. Kay mentioned her name to me, but we've never met.'

'I was engaged to her once.'

'So Kay told me.'

'Oh, she told you? Well, what she probably didn't tell you was that Linda's the only girl I ever loved, which, considering that she's a brunette, is rather remarkable. I worshipped her, Jerry o' man, and when she gave me the bum's rush, my heart broke and life became a total blank.'

'I'd never noticed it.'

'No, I wear the mask. But you can take it from me that that's what happened. You see before you, Jerry, a broken man with nothing to live for.'

'Except the Pyke millions.'

'Oh, those,' said Biff, dismissing them with a contemptuous wave of the hand. He fell into a moody silence, but it was not long before he was speaking again, this time in more cheerful vein.

'Jerry, o' man.'

'Yes?'

'Shall I tell you something? I've been thinking of Linda, and I've reached a rather interesting conclusion. I believe there's quite a chance that under the present altered conditions the sun may come smiling through again. Now that I've got these millions – an added attraction, as you might say – she may turn things over in her mind and then reconsider.'

'It's possible.'

'Have you studied the sex closely?'

'Not very.'

'I have, and I know that it often happens that a girl who has handed a man his hat and helped him from her presence with a kick in the pants gets a completely different slant on him when she learns that he owns the majority stock in about fifty-seven blue chip corporations. I think that when Linda finds out the score, she'll forgive and forget. Am I right or wrong?'

'Right, I should say, unless you did something particularly out of the way to offend her. What made her hand you your hat?'

'Blondes, Jerry o' man. I was rather festooned in blondes at that time, and she objected – I may say she objected strongly. You know what Linda's like.'

'No, I don't. I've never seen her.'

'Nor you have. I was forgetting. Well, she's one of those calm, quiet girls you'd think nothing would steam up, but she has this in common with a stick of trinitrotoluol, that, given the right conditions, she can explode with a deafening report, strewing ruin and desolation in all directions. She did this when she found me giving supper to a blonde whose name, if I remember correctly, was Mabel. But that was a year ago. A year's a long time, Jerry.'

'It is.'

'She may have changed her mind.'

'Girls have been known to.'

'Especially if I make it clear to her that I'm off blondes for life. Do you know what I'm going to do? I'm going to seek her out and see how she feels about things. The trouble is I don't know her address. She used to have an apartment in Chelsea, but she's not there now and I can't find her name in the telephone book. Short of engaging detectives and bloodhounds, I don't know what to do.'

'Perfectly simple. You say she's Tilbury's niece. Ask Tilbury.'

Biff scratched his chin thoughtfully.

'Between ourselves, o' man, I'm not too eager to meet Tilbury just now.'

'Then ask his secretary. She's bound to know.'

'My God, Jerry, you're shrewd. I'll do just that little thing. I'll go and see the wench immediately. And meanwhile you might be calling Kay up and telling her the good news. And don't forget about that picture. Impress upon her that I need it without delay, or I shan't be able to meet current expenses. I'll write down the number for you. And how about a bite of dinner when I return from seeing the sec?'

'I can't, I'm afraid. I'm dining with my uncle.'

'Take me along.'

'You wouldn't like him. He's a solicitor – Shoesmith, Shoesmith, Shoesmith and Shoesmith, Lincoln's Inn Fields. A man of many sterling qualities, but dry and cold and sarcastic, not your type at all. Well, if you want to catch that secretary, you'd better be hurrying, or she'll have gone before you get there.'

'Starting immediately. Tell me, where is this Tilbury House?'

'Halfway down Fleet Street.'

'You don't think there's any danger that Tilbury will be lurking in his office as late as this?'

'He probably left hours ago. Why don't you want to meet him?'

'I'll tell you. Have you noticed a peculiar thing as you go through life, Jerry? I allude to the fact that whatever you do, you can't please everybody. Take the present case. Edmund Biffen Pyke's testimentary dispositions or whatever you call them have made me all smiles, but I greatly fear they will have administered a nasty jolt to Tilbury. He was the old boy's brother and must have expected to gather in a substantial portion of the kitty, if not the whole works, and I can see him taking the thing a bit hard. If he's had the news, the sight of me might well give him a stroke. Still, he's loaded with the stuff, so this little extra bit ought not really to matter to him. There's always a bright side,' said Biff, and on this philosophical note took his departure.

Left alone, Jerry lost no time in calling the number Biff had given him. The prospect of hearing Kay's voice again was one that appealed to him strongly.

'Kay?' he said some minutes later.

The voice that replied was not Kay's. It was that of Henry Blake-Somerset.

'Who is this?'

'Oh, hullo, Mr Blake-Somerset. This is Jerry Shoesmith. Can I speak to Miss Christopher?'

'Miss Christopher is not in,' said Henry, as frigidly as if he were refusing some doubtful character a visa.

This was not strictly true, for she was in the next room dressing for dinner, but he was in no mood to be fussy about the truth. He was thinking the worst. He had been suspicious about his betrothed's relations with this Shoesmith fellow ever since she and he had appeared at his door on what were obviously excellent terms, and this telephone call – this sinister, secret, surreptitious telephone call – had cemented those suspicions. There was a cold gleam in his pale eyes as he banged the receiver back into its place.

Kay came out of the bedroom, all dressed up.

'Who was that on the phone?' she asked.

'Wrong number,' said Henry.

CHAPTER FOUR

THE Tilbury of whom mention has been made from time to time in this chronicle, the employer of Jerry Shoesmith and William Albert Pilbeam's niece Gwendoline Gibbs, should more properly have been alluded to as Lord Tilbury, for it was several years now since a gracious sovereign, as a reward for flooding Great Britain with some of the most repellent daily, weekly and monthly periodicals seen around since Caxton's invention of the printing press, had bestowed on him a Barony. He was the founder and proprietor of the Mammoth Publishing Company, and at the moment when Jerry and Biff's reunion had taken place he was in his office at Tilbury House dictating letters to Gwendoline Gibbs. And it may be said at once that he was doing it with the love-light in his eyes and in a voice which a poet would have had no hesitation in comparing to that of a turtle dove calling to its mate.

Lord Tilbury was short, stout and inclined to come out in spots if he ate lobster, but there is no law prohibiting short, stout Press lords, even when spotty, from falling in love with willowy blondes, and there were few blondes more willowy than Gwendoline. He was, moreover, at what is sometimes called the dangerous age, the age of those Pittsburgh millionaires who are so prone to marry into musical comedy choruses.

He was a widower. In the days when he had been plain George Pyke, long before he had even founded *Society Spice*, the first of his numerous enterprises, he had married a colourless young woman of the name of Lucy Maynard, and when after a year or two of marriage she had drifted colourlessly out of his life, it had never occurred to him to look about him for a replacement. His work absorbed him, and he felt no need for feminine companionship other than that of his niece Linda Rome, who kept house for him at his mansion on Wimbledon Common.

And then the agency had sent him Gwendoline Gibbs, and it was as if one of his many employees who were always saying to one another that what the old son of a bachelor needed was to have a bomb touched off under him had proceeded from words to action. He looked forward eagerly to the time when, with her at his side, he would take his annual holiday on the yacht which ought at any moment to be in readiness at Cannes. Meanwhile, he dictated letters to her.

The one he was dictating now was to the editor of *Society Spice*, whose work, he considered, lacked zip and ginger. *Society Spice* had once been edited by Mr Pilbeam's son Percy, and under his guidance had reached a high pitch of excellence with a new scandal featured almost every week. But Percy was shrewd and he saw no reason why he should nose out people's discreditable secrets for a salary from Tilbury House when he would be doing far better for himself nosing them out on his own behalf. He had resigned, borrowed a little capital and started a private investigation agency, and Lord Tilbury had never ceased to regret his loss. None of his successors had had the Pilbeam touch, and this latest man – Shoesmith, his name was – was the least satisfactory of the lot.

He finished dictating the note, its acerbity causing Gwendoline to label it mentally as a stinker, and when the last harsh word had been spoken returned to his melting mood.

'I hope I am not tiring you, Miss Gibbs,' he said tenderly.

'Oh, no, Lord Tilbury.'

'I am sure you must be tired,' his lordship insisted. 'It is this muggy weather. You had better go home and lie down.'

Gwendoline assured him that his kindness was greatly appreciated, but said that she had a dinner date for that night and would have to wait till her cavalier arrived to pick her up.

'My cousin,' she said, and Lord Tilbury, who had writhed in a spasm of jealousy, stopped writhing. He had no objection to cousins.

'I see,' he said, relieved. 'Then would you mind putting in a New York telephone call for me.'

'Yes, Lord Tilbury.'

'What would be the time in New York?'

Gwendoline made a rapid calculation, and said that it would be about twelve-thirty.

'Then I ought just to catch Mr Haskell before he goes to lunch. The call is to Haskell and Green. They are a legal firm. Ask for a person to person call to Mr Leonard Haskell.'

'Yes, Lord Tilbury.'

'The number is Murray Hill 2-4025. Oh, and, Miss Gibbs, you sent that marconigram to Mr Llewellyn's boat?'

'Yes, Lord Tilbury.'

The door closed, and Lord Tilbury fell into a reverie, thinking of this and that, but principally of Gwendoline Gibb's profile, which he had been studying with loving care for the past half hour. He was in the process of trying to decide whether she was seen to greater advantage side face or full face, when the door opened and a girl came in. And he was about to ask her how she dared enter the presence without making an appointment and – worse – without knocking, when he saw that it was his niece, Linda Rome.

In comparison with Gwendoline Gibbs, Linda Rome could not have been called beautiful, but she was an attractive girl with clear eyes and a wide and goodhumoured mouth. Kay had described her to Jerry as sensible, and it was this quality perhaps that stood out most in her appearance. She looked capable and, as Mr Gish of the Gish Galleries in Bond Street, where she worked, would have testified. she was extremely capable. Soothing, too, was another adjective that could have been applied to her, though her advent seemed to have irritated Lord Tilbury. There was suppressed annoyance in his manner as he eyed her.

'Yes?' he said. 'Yes, Linda, what is it?'

'Am I interrupting you?'

'Yes,' said Lord Tilbury, who did not believe in formal courtesy between uncle and niece. 'I am making a telephone call to New York.'

'I'm sorry. I only looked in to tell you that I've fixed us up with rooms at Barribault's. With so little time before you'll be off on your yacht trip, it didn't seem worth while engaging a new staff.'

There had recently been a volcanic upheaval at The Oaks, Wimbledon Common, with Lord Tilbury in one of his most imperious moods falling foul of and denouncing his domestic helpers and the helpers resigning their portfolios in a body: and Linda in her sensible way had decided that the only thing to do was to move temporarily to a hotel.

'You're on the third floor, I'm on the fourth. We shall be quite comfortable.'

'For how long? It may be for weeks.'

'No, that's all right. After you left this morning a phone call came from the skipper of the yacht. Apparently whatever was wrong with the poor thing's insides has been put right, and he says you can start your cruise any time you want to.'

'Good. I wish I could start tomorrow, but unfortunately Ivor Llewellyn is on his way over from New York and I shall have to be here to give him lunch. It's a great nuisance, but unavoidable.'

'Who's Ivor Llewellyn?'

'Motion picture man. Big advertiser. I can't afford to offend him. And now, if you don't mind, Linda, I am making this important telephone call to New York.'

'To Mr Llewellyn?'

'No, he's on the *Queen Mary*. This is to Edmund's lawyers.'

'Oh, about the will?'

'Precisely.'

'I must wait to hear that. I wonder if he's left his money to you.'

'I can think of no one else to whom he could leave it. We were never on very close terms, but he was my elder brother.'

'How about charities?'

'He did not approve of charities.'

'Then you ought to collect. Though why you want any more money beats me. Haven't you enough already?'

'Don't be silly,' said Lord Tilbury, who disliked foolish questions. 'Ah!'

The telephone had rung. His hand darted at the receiver like a striking snake.

'Mr Haskell? ... How do you do? ... This is Lord Tilbury of the Mammoth Publishing Company. I understand you are handling the estate of my brother Edmund Biffen Pyke ...'

For some moments his lordship's share in the conversation was confined to greetings and civilities. Then, getting down to it like a good business man, he asked to be informed of the contents of Edmund Biffen Pyke's will, and for perhaps half a minute sat listening in silence. At the end of that period he broke it abruptly.

'WHAT!!' he roared in a voice that caused his niece to jump at least two inches. When she returned to earth, the ejaculation still seemed to be echoing through the room, and she was conscious of a mild surprise that plaster had not fallen from the ceiling.

Surprise was followed by alarm. Lord Tilbury's face had taken on a purple tinge and his breathing was stertorous.

'Uncle George!' she cried. 'What is it?'

But she was an intelligent girl and did not really need to ask the question. It was plain to her that the news that had been wafted across the Atlantic had not been good news and that it was no inheritor of millions who sat spluttering before her.

'Can I get you a glass of water?'

'Water!' gurgled Lord Tilbury, and you could tell by his manner that he thought poorly of the stuff. 'Do you know –'

'What?'

'Do you know – ?'

'Yes?'

'Do you know who he's left his money to?' demanded Lord Tilbury, becoming coherent. 'That young waster Christopher!'

He had expected the information to astound her, and it did.

'To *Biff*?'

'You heard me.'

'But Biff always gave me the idea that he and Uncle Edmund were hardly on speaking terms. What on earth made him do that?'

Lord Tilbury did not answer. He was staring before him in a sandbagged manner that spoke of an overwrought soul, and it seemed to Linda the tactful thing to leave this stricken man to his grief.

She moved to the door, and went out.

2

A few minutes later Lord Tilbury, too, took his departure, en route for his club, where he could obtain the stiff drink he so sorely needed. His preoccupation was so great that he passed Gwendoline Gibbs in the outer office without a word or a look. This was very unusual, and it puzzled Gwendoline. She was not a girl who as a rule thought for any length of time about anything except motion pictures and hair do's, but she found herself meditating now on her employer with what for her was a good deal of intensity.

Lord Tilbury's emotional state of mind had not passed unnnoticed by her. She had discussed it with her cousin Percy, and he had confirmed her impression that all those tender glances and all that solicitude for her welfare were significant. It would not be the first time, said Percy, that a middle-aged widower had become enamoured of his secretary. His father, Mr Pilbeam senior, had once told him that half the couples who came to Barribault's Hotel were elderly business men who had married their secretaries. It was propinquity that did it, he said, the working with them all day and every day in the same office.

Her own reading had convinced her of the truth of this. In her capacity of secretary to the head of Tilbury House she got all the firm's publications free, and in many of these such as *Cupid, Romance Weekly* and the rest of them it was common form for the rich man to marry the poor but beautiful girl. She could think offhand of a dozen such unions which she had come across in the course of her studies.

A dreamy look came into her eyes, and if she was wishing that her employer could have been a little younger and a good deal slimmer and altogether more like Captain Eric Frobisher of the Guards, the one who married the governess, she was also thinking that a girl could do far worse than link her lot with his. She had just written the words 'Lady Tilbury' in her notebook, to see how they looked, when the door opened and Biff appeared.

Biff came in with a jaunty stride, as befitted a newly made millionaire, but at the sight of Gwendoline he halted abruptly, rocked back on his heels and stood staring at her, speechless.

It is a peculiar thing about female beauty, and one on which thoughtful men have often commented, that you never can tell where it is going to pop up, except of course on the cover of *Society Spice*, where it appears with monotonous regularity each week, usually in step-ins or a bikini bathing suit. Nobody acquainted with the late Alexander Gibbs and his late wife Amelia would have supposed them capable of producing a daughter guaranteed to stupefy strong men at a dozen paces, but they had done it. Neither of her parents could ever have achieved success even in a seaside beauty contest, but Gwendoline's outer crust was sensational. Her eyes were a Mediterranean blue, her hair as golden as the best butter, and her face the face that launched a thousand ships and burned the topless towers of Ilium.

To describe Biff as impressed would be an understatement.

'Hi!' he said, when able to speak.

'Good evening,' said Gwendoline. 'Are you looking for someone?'

'Not now I've found you,' said Biff, who prided himself on the swiftness of his work. The odd breathless feeling which had paralysed his vocal cords had subsided, and he was his old debonair self again. The mission on which he had come, the quest for Linda Rome's address, had passed completely from his mind.

'If you are,' said Gwendoline, ignoring the remark, which she considered in dubious taste and bordering on the fresh, 'you've come too late. There isn't anybody here.'

'Just as I would have arranged it, if I'd been consulted. Old piefaced Tilbury not around?'

'If you are alluding to my employ-ah, he left half an hour ago.'

Biff nodded understandingly.

'That's always the way. Everybody works but Father. I've never known one of these tycoons who wasn't a clock-watcher. So he sneaks off, does he, and leaves you at your post? Poor, faithful little soul. You, I take it, are his right-hand woman?'

'I am his secretary.'

'That's just your modest way of putting it. I'll bet you really run the show. Without you, the Mammoth Publishing Company would go pop and cease to exist, and what a break that would be for everybody. But it's a shame. You're wasted here. You ought to be in the movies.'

Gwendoline's haughtiness fell from her like a garment. This was the way she liked people to talk. Her azure eyes glowed, and for the first time she allowed herself to smile.

'Do you really think so?'

'I do indeed.'

'Quite a number of my friends have told me the same thing.'

'I'm not surprised.'

'There's a big movie man, Mr Ivor Llewellyn, coming here in a day or two. I'm hoping he'll think so, too.'

'I know Ivor Llewellyn. I interviewed him once.'

'What's he like?'

'A hippopotamus. You think he may give you a job?'

'I wish he would. I'd love to be in pictures.'

'Pix, I believe, is the more correct term. Well, I shall watch your career with considerable interest. In my opinion you will go far. If I may say so, you have that thing, that certain thing, that makes the birds forget to sing. Arising from which, how do you react to the idea of letting me buy you a few cents' worth of dinner?'

Gwendoline had made a discovery.

'You're American, aren't you?'

'Not only American, but one of the Americans who have made the country great. Well, how about a bite?'

'I'm waiting for Percy.'

'That sounds like the title of one of those avant-garde off-Broadway shows. Who's Percy?'

'My cousin. He's taking me to dinner, but he's late. I suppose he's out on a case.'

'Out on a what?'

'He runs an investigation agency.'

'You mean he's a private eye?' said Biff, intrigued. 'Now there's a thing I'd have liked to be. The fifth of bourbon in the desk drawer, the automatic in the holster and the lightly clad secretary on the lap. Yes, I've often wished I were a shamus.'

'What are you?'

'Me?' Biff flicked a speck of dust from his coat sleeve. 'Oh, I'm a millionaire.'

'And I'm the Queen of Sheba.'

Biff shook his head.

'The Queen of Sheba was a brunette. You're more the Helen of Troy type. Not that Helen of Troy was in your class. You begin where she left off.'

Gwendoline's initial feeling of hostility towards this intruder had now vanished completely.

'No kidding,' she said. 'Are you really a millionaire?'

'Sure. Ask the waiter on the third floor at Barribault's. Name of Pilbeam.'

Gwendoline uttered a ladylike squeal.

'Why, that's my uncle.'

'This seems to bring us very close together.'

'Is your name Christopher?'

'Edmund Biffen Christopher.'

'I was lunching with Uncle Willie this morning, and he told me all about you. He said he was there when a cable came saying you had come into millions.'

'That's right.'

'Cool'

'What he said, as I recall, was "Cor lumme!", but I imagine the two expressions mean about the same thing. Yes, your Uncle Willie was giving me breakfast when the story broke, and if he gives me breakfast, it seems only fair that I should give you dinner. Reciprocity, it's called. And another aspect of the matter. Don't overlook the fact that these private eyes have to watch the pennies. This Percy of yours is probably planning to take you to the Popular Café and push meat loaf and cocoa into you. With me, it'll be the Savoy Grill and what you'll get will be caviar to start with and, to follow, whatever you may select from the bill of fare, paying no attention whatsoever to the prices in the right-hand column. The whole washed down with some nourishing wine that foams at the mouth when the waiter takes the cork out. Grab your hat and come along.'

Gwendoline, though her eyes glowed at the picture he had conjured up, remained firm.

'We can't go without Percy.'

'To hell, if I may use the expression, with Percy. Stand him up.'

'Certainly not. I can't hurt his feelings.'

'Okay,' said Biff amiably. It had occurred to him that it might be interesting to meet the head of a private enquiry agency and learn all that went on in a concern like that. Probably this Percy would prove to have a fund of good stories about dope rings, spy rings, Maharajah's rubies and what not. It was odd, though, that stuff about hurting his feelings. He had not known till then that private eyes had any feelings.

3

Jerry had managed to get away reasonably early from his dinner with his Uncle John, and it was with relief that he reached home and settled himself in the one comfortable chair Number Three, Halsey Chambers possessed, for Mr Shoesmith was never a very entertaining host and an evening with him always had a depleting effect. He mixed himself a whisky and soda, far stronger than Henry Blake-Somerset would have approved, and fell to thinking how pleasant it would be if someone were to leave him nine or ten millions. He tried not to envy Biff, but he could not help wishing that there were more godfathers like the late E. B. Pyke around. His own had been content to fulfil his obligations with a small silver mug.

He also thought of Kay and of Henry Blake-Somerset and wondered once again what had induced that lovely and intelligent girl to commit herself to marriage with a man like that. He had not seen a great deal of Henry Blake-Somerset, but what little he had seen had been enough to tell him that nothing but unhappiness could result from such a union. It was his duty, he felt, to save her, and he was resolved to omit no act or word to that end.

He then mused on Biff, speculating idly as to how he was passing the evening. From his knowledge of him he presumed that he was celebrating, and he knew that when Edmund Biffen Christopher celebrated, he left no stone unturned.

His meditations were interrupted by the clicking of a key in the front door, the falling with a crash of something that sounded like the hatstand in the hall and a sharp yelp of agony from, he supposed, Biff, on whose toes the object had apparently descended. The next moment Biff entered, followed by a pimpled young man who was a stranger to Jerry.

'Hi, Jerry,' he said.

He spoke so thickly and was weaving so noticeably in his walk that Jerry was able to form an instant diagnosis.

'Biff, you're blotto!'

'And why not?' said Biff warmly. He made a movement to seat himself, missed the chair by some inches and continued his remarks from the floor. 'You don't become a millionaire every day, do you? And it's a poor heart that never rejoices, isn't it? You can take it from me, Jerry o' man, that if a fellow raised from rags to riches at the breakfast table isn't tanked to the uvula by nightfall, it simply means he hasn't been trying. Meet my friend Percy Pilbeam.'

His friend Percy Pilbeam was a singularly uninviting young man of about Biff's age. His eyes were too small and too close together and he marcelled his hair in a manner distressing to right-thinking people, besides having side whiskers and a small and revolting moustache. He looked to Jerry like something unpleasant out of an early Evelyn Waugh novel, and he took as instant a dislike to him as he had taken to Henry Blake-Somerset.

'He's a private eye,' said Biff. 'Runs the Argus Enquiry Agency. Makes his living measuring footprints and picking up small objects from the carpet and placing them carefully in envelopes. Get him to tell you some time how he secured the necessary evidence in the case of Nicholson versus Nicholson, Hibbs, Alsopp, Bunter, Frobisher, Davenport and others. Well, see you later, o' man,' he said, rising with some difficulty and weaving into his bedroom. 'Got to freshen up a bit.'

Percy Pilbeam uttered a brief snigger and gave his moustache a twirl.

'What a night!' he said.

'I can imagine,' said Jerry aloofly.

'Glad I managed to get him home all right.'

'Can't have been easy.'

'It wasn't. He's the sort that gets fractious after he's had a few. He wanted to fight the policeman on the corner. I hauled him away.'

'Very good of you.'

'Does he often carry on like that?'

'He was rather apt to when I knew him in New York.'

'Odd how drink affects people so differently. I know a man – fellow named Murphy – Fleet Street chap – who gets more and more amiable the more he puts away. He can shift the stuff all night and never turn a hair.'

'It's a gift.'

'I suppose so. Well, I'll be pushing along. Glad to have met you. Good night,' said Percy Pilbeam.

Jerry went to the door of Biff's room. Biff was at the basin, sponging his face. If ever there was an ideal moment for talking to him like a Dutch uncle, this was it, but Jerry let it pass.

'Ah,' he said, relieved. 'Going to bed, eh? Quite right. Best place in the world for you. Go to sleep and dream of tomorrow's hangover.'

Biff's dripping face rose from the basin wearing a look of amazement and incredulity.

'Going to bed? Of course I'm not going to bed. Just freshening up. I'm off in a moment to sock a cop.'

'Do *what?*'

'Sock a cop.'

'Oh, come,' said Jerry pacifically. 'You don't want to sock a cop.'

Biff thought this over as he plied the towel.

'It's not so much a question of *wanting* to sock a cop. It's more that I feel my pride demands it. Do you know the cop on the corner with the ginger moustache?'

'I've seen him.'

'He's the one I've got to teach a sharp lesson to. As I was entering Halsey Court, he cautioned me. Cautioned me, Jerry o' man. Said I was plastered and *cautioned* me. We Christophers don't take that sort of thing lying down.'

'Were you lying down?'

'Certainly not. Standing as straight as an arrow with my chin up and both feet on the ground. The only possible thing the man could have cavilled at was that I was singing. And why shouldn't I sing? This is a free country, isn't it?'

'No.'

'Well, that's the way I always heard the story. How about Magna Charta?'

'What about it?'

'If I remember rightly, Magna Charta specifically lays it down that you can sing all you want to, sing all over the countryside like a linnet in Spring. Stands to reason those Barons who made King what's-his-name sign on the dotted line wouldn't have overlooked a point like that. You know what's wrong with the world today? Not enough singing.

67

And the moment you start opening your mouth, along comes some ginger-moustached flatty and cautions you. Well, I propose to blot this flatty from the London scene. Do you know what he'll rue? The day he was born, that's what he'll rue. Treat the Christophers with ordinary civility and they're suavity itself, but anyone who asks for trouble gets it in full measure.'

'Oh, go to bed, Biff.'

'Can't be done, Jerry o' man. No turning back now. My regiment leaves at dawn.'

'What do you think Kay will say if you get jugged?'

'She'll be proud of me.'

'Have you reflected that this policeman may have a wife and children?'

'He has a ginger moustache.'

'But isn't it possible that he may have a wife and children as well?'

'I guess so, but he should have remembered that earlier,' said Biff sternly, and Jerry closed the door and turned away. A few moments later its handle rattled and a stentorian 'Hey!' came through the woodwork.

'Now what?' said Jerry.

'I can't get out.'

'No, I noticed that.'

'You've locked me in!'

'Just the Shoesmith service,' said Jerry and made for his own room, feeling that he had done a knightly deed on Kay's behalf. His great love had made him come to look on this deplorable brother of hers as a sacred trust.

CHAPTER FIVE

THE cubbyhole allotted to Jerry at Tilbury House was two floors down from the head of the firm's palatial office, and many people would have thought it unfit for human habitation. Jerry was one of them. Its ink-stained furniture and evil-smelling stuffiness always lowered his spirits. It was not easy in such surroundings to concentrate on uncongenial work, and when towards noon on the following morning the door handle turned, indicating that someone was about to enter and take his mind off *Society Spice*, he welcomed the interruption. A boy came in, bearing one of those forms which visitors have to fill up before they can approach even the humblest Tilbury House editor.

It ran:

Visitor's Name	E. B. Christopher
To see	Editor of *Society Spice*
Business	Terrifically urgent, Jerry old man. Drop everything and confer with me without a moment's delay.

'Send him in,' said Jerry, and a few moments later Biff appeared, and he braced himself for rebukes and recriminations. The haughty spirit of the Christophers would, he knew, have been bound to resent being immured in bedrooms. Before leaving Halsey Chambers he had unlocked Biff's door, but he felt that this would have done little to alleviate his guest's pique.

To his surprise, Biff seemed to be in no hostile mood. His manner was grave, but not unfriendly. He said 'Gosh, what a lousy office,' dusted a chair and sat down.

'Jerry o' man,' he said, 'I would like you, if you will, to throw your mind back to last night. Tell me in a few simple words what happened.'

69

Jerry found no difficulty in recapitulating the facts. They were graven on his memory.

'You were tight.'

'Sure, sure. We can take that as read. And what occurred?'

'You staggered in, accompanied by a weird object of the name of Pickford or something like that.'

'Pilbeam. Most interesting fellow. Runs a private enquiry agency and obtains the necessary evidence. What happened then?'

'You expressed a wish to go out again and sock the policeman on the corner.'

'And then?'

'I locked you in your room.'

Biff nodded.

'I thought I had the story sequence correctly. Well, let me tell you, Jerry o' man, that you did me a signal service. I will go further. You saved my life. The United States Marines never put up a smoother job. Do you know what would have been the outcome if you hadn't shown a presence of mind which it is impossible to overpraise? Ruin, desolation and despair, that's what the outcome would have been. That cop would have pinched me.'

Jerry agreed that this was what almost certainly would have occurred, but was unable to understand why a seasoned veteran of arrests like Biff should attach such importance to what by this time he might have been expected to have come to regard as mere routine.

'Well, weren't you always getting pinched in New York?' he said, putting this point.

'I was,' said Biff, 'but the difference between me getting pinched in the old home town three years ago and being thrown into a dungeon below the castle moat in London as of even date is subtle but well-marked, Jerry o' man. Three years ago, had I been escorted to the coop, it would have set me back some trivial sum like ten bucks. Today it would be more like ten million.'

'I don't follow you.'

'You will,' said Biff. He took a paper from his pocket. 'Do you know what this is?'

'It looks like a letter.'

'And it is a letter. From the New York lawyers. I picked it up at Barribault's just now, and do you know what I did when I read it? I reeled.'

'Just like last night.'

Biff gave him a reproving look that said that this was no time for frivolity. His face was grave.

'Never mind about last night, it's today we've got to concentrate on. Where was I?'

'Reeling.'

'Ah yes. And if ever anyone was entitled to reel, it was me. You remember the bit at the end of the cable about me getting old Pyke's money in accordance with the provisions of the Trust and letter follows?'

'I remember. This is the letter?'

'Nothing but. They said it would follow and it followed, and you can take it from me that it's dynamite. Shall I tell you about the Trust I've got to act in accordance with the provisions of? They call it a Spendthrift Trust, which is a pretty offensive way of putting it, to start with, and when you've heard what a Spendthrift Trust is, you'll be astounded that Edmund Biffen Pyke should have countenanced such a thing. As dirty a trick to play on a young fellow trying to get along as I ever heard of. Briefly, the way it works out is that the trustees stick to the money like Scotch tape, and I don't get a smell of it till I'm thirty.'

'Well, that's not so long to wait. Aren't you nearly that?'

'Pretty nearly. In about another week.'

'Then what are you worrying about?'

'I'll tell you what I'm worrying about. You haven't heard the snapper. The provisions of this Spendthift Trust are that if I'm arrested for any misdemeanour before my thirtieth birthday, I don't get a nickel.'

The look which he directed at Jerry as he spoke made it plain that he was expecting his words to have a stirring effect, and he was not disappointed. Jerry jumped as if the chair he sat in had suddenly become incandescent. He could not have shown more consternation if it had been his own fortune that had thus been placed in jeopardy.

'Good Lord!' he cried.

'I thought that would make you sit up,' said Biff with a certain gloomy satisfaction.

'You're sure you've got your facts right?'

'Sure I'm sure. It's all in the letter. Couched, if that's the word, in legal phraseology, but perfectly clear. Didn't I tell you I was certain there was bound to be a catch somewhere?'

'When did your godfather make this will?'

'Three years ago, just about the time I was leaving for Paris.'

'And he never said a word to you about it?'

'Not a word. That's what makes me so sore. Can you imagine a man playing a low-down trick like that, just letting me amble along doing what comes naturally and then springing it on me that if I'd been a better boy, I'd have cleaned up but, as it is, I get nothing. It shatters one's whole faith in mankind.'

'Didn't he even drop a hint?'

'If you could call it a hint. I saw him before I left, and he told me to keep out of trouble when I was in Paris, and I said I would, and he said I'd better.'

'That was all?'

'That's all there was, there wasn't any more.'

'He must have been an odd sort of man.'

'He was.'

Silence fell on the editorial offices of *Society Spice*. Biff scowled at the strip of linoleum which was Tilbury House's idea of a carpet for junior editors, while Jerry stared dumbly at a photograph of a young person apparently in the final stages of a strip tease, one of three on which he had been trying to decide for next week's *Spice*'s cover. It was he who spoke first.

'This is pretty serious, Biff.'

'You're telling me!'

'You really lose all the money if you're arrested?'

'No question about it.'

'You'd better not get arrested.'

'Yes, I thought of that.'

A horrible possibility occurred to Jerry.

'Have you been arrested since you came to Paris?'

Biff was able to reassure him there.

'Oddly enough, no. The cops aren't nearly so fussy in Paris as they are in New York. There's much more of the live and let live spirit. But my blood runs cold when I think how near I came to it only a few days ago. There was some unpleasantness in a bar, and I socked an agent de ville. That's why I moved to London. To get away from it all, if you follow me.'

'But you weren't pinched?'

'No, he hadn't time to pinch me.'

'Well, you will be if you start doing that sort of thing here. It's a pity you have this urge to punch policemen.'

'It's just a mannerism.'

'I'd correct it, if I were you.'

'I will. I've learned my lesson. Well, you see now, Jerry o' man, why I'm so grateful to you for what you did last night. But for you, I would now be inside looking out, and a letter would be following to say I could kiss my heritage goodbye. Think back, and you will recall that I used the expression "You saved my life". I repeat it. How can I ever repay you?'

'I don't want to be repaid.'

'Of course you do. Everybody wants repaying. Jerry o' man, you simply must let me give you that twenty thousand.'

'No.'

'Well, lend it to you, then.'

'No.'

Biff frowned at the linoleum.

'I must say I don't like the way you're refusing to enter into the spirit of the thing. Have you nothing to suggest? I know. I'll back your play.'

'What play?'

'Haven't you written a play? I thought everyone had.'

'Not me. I've been too busy editing this ghastly paper.'

'Editing! That word puts me on the right track. How would you like to edit something worth while?'

'I'd love it.'

'Then here's what we're going to do. I'll start a paper and you shall run it.'

'It costs a fortune starting a paper from scratch.'

'Suppose I bought a going concern.'

Jerry gave a little jump. This was opening up a new line of thought.

'Do you really mean it, Biff?'

'Of course I mean it. What do you think I meant? Do you know of any going concerns?'

'Did you ever hear of the *Thursday Review*?'

'Vaguely. A pal of mine in Paris takes it in. It's politics and literature and all that slop, isn't it?'

'That sort of thing. I've had one or two pieces in it.'

'Why do you bring it up?'

'Because I heard the other day that the editor was retiring, and I'd give anything to take on his job. It's right in my line. But what's the good of talking about it? The syndicate that owns it would sell, I suppose, if the price was high enough, but it would cost the earth.'

'Well, I've got the earth, or I shall have in another week, always provided I stay out of the calaboose. And you can take it from me, Jerry o' man, that staying out of calabooses is what from now on I'm going to specialize in.'

Jerry drummed on the desk with his fingers. He looked at the photograph of the strip tease artist and seemed to draw encouragement from it.

'I'll tell you something, Biff. Actually I don't think you'd be risking much. The *Thursday's* always made money, and I don't believe I'd let you down. And yet ... I don't know.'

Biff would have none of this cat-in-the-adage spirit. He was all enthusiasm.

'I do. Consider it done. I have the utmost confidence in your ability to make the damn thing the talk of the intelligentsia, and don't worry about the syndicate not wanting to sell. I know these syndicates. Once they hear there's somebody ready to put up real cash, they're after him like Percy Pilbeam on the track of the necessary evidence. By the way, did you know that Percy used to edit *Society Spice*?'

'No, I never heard that.'

74

'Fact. He told me last night.'

'He looks as if he would have been the ideal editor.'

'He was, so he tells me. He spoke very highly of himself. He doesn't think much of you as a successor. He thinks you fall short in the way of dishing the dirt.'

'I've an idea my lord Tilbury feels the same.'

'Well, to hell with old Tilbury and to hell with Percy Pilbeam. Harking back to this *Thursday Review* thing, I'll start the negotiations right away, and your trouser-seat will be warming the editorial chair before you know where you are.'

Jerry sat speechless, looking into the future. It seemed to open before him in a golden vista, and if the thought presented itself that the whole of that future depended on Biff keeping out of the clutches of the law, it was succeeded by the comforting reflection that he had got to do so only for another week. Even Biff, he felt, possibly a little too optimistically, could probably do that.

'I don't know what to say,' he said. 'You've rather taken my breath away. I'd like to try to thank you—'

'Don't give it a thought.'

Jerry laughed.

'That expression seems to run in the family. It was what Kay said to me when I thanked her for standing me a cup of coffee. Kay!' he exclaimed. 'I was forgetting her. I tried to phone her last night, but she was out and all I got was Henry Blake-Somerset. Do you realize that she doesn't know a thing about what's happened? Unless you told her?'

'Oh, I told her. I called her up last night from one of the bars into which Percy Pilbeam led me, though it is possible, of course, that I was leading him. I explained the whole set-up.'

'Was she thrilled?'

'I think she would have been, if she had grasped the gist. But she didn't. She kept telling me she couldn't understand a word I was saying and accused me – with some justice, I admit – of being under the influence of the sauce. She then hung up. I was annoyed at the time, but I can see now that my articulation may not have been as clear as I could have wished. I seem to remember slurring my words a little.'

'So she doesn't know?'

'Hasn't a notion. Nor is she aware that I've got to have that picture. The need is pressing. All sorts of new expenses have cropped up, and I can't waste time waiting for her to mail me the thing. It'll have to be fetched. Not by me, because I can't go to Paris myself – that trouble with the constabulary I spoke of – so everything points to you. You'll have to pop over there. How are you fixed for cash?'

'I've enough. And I ought to go to Paris anyway to pick up those keys and get my things. My uncle was fussing a good deal about his keys last night. But how can I manage it when I'm tied down here?'

'Won't Tilbury let you off?'

'After I've just had my holiday? No.'

'You could ask him.'

'No, I couldn't.'

'Then we seem to be faced with what you might call a dilemma.'

'We are.'

There was a knock at the door. A boy entered, bearing a letter. Jerry opened the envelope, and laughed.

'Correction,' he said. 'Tilbury says he *will* let me off.'

'Eh?'

'And I'm not tied down here. This is from the big chief, dispensing with my services.'

'He's fired you?'

'As of today.'

'Well, the old popeyed son of a what not,' said Biff. 'Still, it just shows what I've always said, that there's a solution for every problem.'

2

The door bell of 16 Rue Jacob, Paris 6, Arrondissement Luxembourg, rang in the asthmatic way it had, and Kay came out of her bedroom to answer it, conscious of a sudden chill. This, she presumed, was Henry Blake-Somerset come to pick her up and take her to lunch to meet his mother, who was passing through Paris on her way to the Riviera, and some sixth sense told her that she was not going to enjoy the experience. She had seen a photograph of Lady Blake-Somerset in Henry's apartment and had been struck by the closeness of her resemblance to Queen Elizabeth the First of England. It is pretty generally conceded that, whatever her numerous merits, there was that about Good Queen Bess which made it difficult for strangers to feel at their ease with her, and she wished Henry had forgotten all about this luncheon date. An idle wish, for Henry never forgot anything.

But it was not he who stood without. It was a large young man with reddish hair, at the sight of whom her heart gave a leap quite unsuitable in a heart which should have leaped only at the sight of her betrothed.

'Jerry!' she cried. 'Well, for heaven's sake! The last person I expected. What are you doing over here?'

'Business trip,' said Jerry briefly. He was resolved to bank down the fire within him and to conduct this interview on orderly, unemotional lines. Just seeing her had caused his own heart to skip like the high hills, but he quickly got it under control, though it was like having to discourage a large, exuberant, bounding dog. 'I came to get those keys at the Lost Property Office and collect the things I'd left in my uncle's apartment. And Biff asked me to come and see you because he wants me to take back a picture of his. He said you would know the one he meant.'

'He's only got one. He isn't a collector. Why does he want it?'

'He's running short of money and wants to sell it. May I come in?'

'I wasn't planning to keep you standing on the mat. Come right in and tell me all your news.'

'I don't know how much you've heard of it,' said Jerry, seating himself. 'Biff tells me he talked to you on the phone.'

Kay laughed and, as always when she did this, Jerry was aware of a sensation similar to, but more pleasurable than, that experienced by the occupant of the electric chair at

Sing-Sing when willing hands turn on the juice.

'In a way he did,' she said, 'but it was more like gargling. He had plainly been looking on the wine when it was red. I couldn't understand more than about one word in twenty, but I seemed to gather that Mr Pyke had left him something, which was better than I had expected. Did he tell you how much?'

'He's left him everything.'

Kay stared.

'What do you mean?'

'Just that.'

'But it sounds as if you were saying that Mr Pyke had left him all his money, which doesn't make sense.'

'He did.'

'You mean ... You can't mean that Biff's a millionaire?'

'That's right.'

Kay raised a finger and stilled an upper lip which was trembling. Amazement, enlarging her eyes, became her so well that Jerry began to have doubts as to his ability to keep the interview orderly and unemotional.

'Say it again – slowly.'

'Biff gets everything.'

'Slower than that. I want to savour each syllable.'

'He's a millionaire.'

'You wouldn't fool me?'

'Certainly not.'

'It's really true?'

'Quite true.'

'Zowie!' said Kay, not having William Albert Pilbeam's familiarity with the expression 'Cor lumme'. There was a tender look in her eyes as she thought of this local boy who had made good. The escapades which in the past had so often caused her to talk to him like a Dutch aunt were forgotten. 'No wonder he was celebrating. After getting pennies from heaven like that, it wouldn't be humane to expect him not to be pie-eyed. Fancy Biff a millionaire! I can hardly believe it. This'll be good news for his circle of acquaintances.'

Jerry nodded.

'That's what I'm afraid of. I warned him that everybody he knew would want their cut.'

'His little sister among the first. What that boy is going to buy for me! There's nothing like having a prosperous millionaire for a brother, especially a generous one like Biff. I may have had occasion to state from time to time that Edmund Biffen Christopher is as crazy as a bed bug and ought to be in some sort of a home, but nobody can say he isn't generous.'

'Not me, anyway. Do you know what was the first thing he said when we met? He wanted to give me twenty thousand pounds.'

'You're kidding.'

'No, it was a firm offer. Naturally I couldn't take it.'

'Why naturally? I know three hundred and forty-seven men in Paris alone who would have jumped at it. Yours must be a wonderful character.'

'I believe Baedeker gives it five stars.'

'The trouble is I still can't quite believe it.'

'That I spurned his gold?'

'No, that he had the gold for you to spurn. Are you *sure* it's true?'

'I saw the cable from the New York lawyers.'

For some moments Kay sat silent. When she spoke, it was to point a moral.

'You know, Jerry, there's a lesson in this for every one of us, and that is that we should always be kind to the very humblest, not that Mr Pyke was that by a long way according to the stories I've heard tell. If Biff hadn't saved the old gentleman's life, I don't suppose this would have happened. Did you know he once saved Mr Pyke's life?'

'No, he never told me that.'

'Our modest hero. It was down at his summer place at Westhampton Beach. He had gone for a swim in the pool much too soon after a big lunch and got cramp and Biff dived in with all his clothes on and gaffed him. No doubt the memory lingered.'

'You think that's the explanation?'

'It must be, because he thoroughly disapproved of Biff's

bohemian revels. He was always having to bail him out after his get-togethers with the police, and it made him as mad as a wet hen. You'd have thought that would have influenced him when he was making his will.'

Jerry stirred uncomfortably. It is never pleasant to have to break bad news.

'It did, I'm afraid.'

'What do you mean?'

As coherently as he could with her eyes boring into him, Jerry revealed the conditions of the Spendthrift Trust, and his heart was torn as he watched the dismay grow in those eyes.

'You mean that if he's arrested, he loses everything?'

'I'm afraid so.'

'One simple tiddly little pinch for doing practically nothing, and he's out millions of dollars?'

'Apparently.'

'But the poor lamb's *always* getting pinched! He can't *help* getting pinched! He'd get pinched somehow if he was alone on a desert island. You ought never to have left him loose in London.'

'I had to. I wanted to see you and tell you to come there at once and help me keep an eye on him. With both of us watching him, he can't get into trouble. I'm flying back this evening. Can you make it, too?'

'But I've a job.'

'Won't they give you a few days off?'

Kay reflected.

'I believe they would if I made a point of it. I'm not an indispensable cog in the machine. But I couldn't come to-day. It would have to be tomorrow at the earliest.'

'Well, that's all right. I think we're safe for the next day or two. It'll take him that long to recover from the shock of that narrow escape he had.'

'What narrow escape?'

Jerry related in as few words as he could manage the salient features of what a writer of tales of suspense would no doubt have called The Case Of The Ginger-Moustached Policeman.

'When I saw him next morning, he was a sobered man. I don't think he would punch a policeman now if you brought one to him asleep on a chair. The Force is safe from him.'

There was an almost worshipping look in Kay's eyes. It was not lost on Jerry. It gave him the idea that if only he could persuade her to join him at lunch, something constructive might result. He had much to say to her in the intimate seclusion of the luncheon table.

'What a mercy you had the presence of mind to lock him in his room. At Barribault's was this?'

'No, he's moved in with me at my flat.'

'Thank heaven for that. It makes me shudder to think of him at large in a place like Barribault's. You'll be able to keep an eye on him.'

'Watch his every move.'

'Well, I don't know how to thank you. I wish there was something I could do for you.'

'There is. Come and have lunch.'

'I can't. I'd love to, but it's impossible. I'm lunching with Henry. And there he is,' said Kay, as an asthmatic tinkle came from the door. 'That must be Henry. He was calling here to pick me up and take me to Armenonville or one of those places.'

It was Henry. He came in, kissed Kay, said he hoped she was ready, as they would have to hurry, and then, seeing Jerry, started like one who perceives a snake in his path.

'Oh, hullo,' he said.

'Hullo,' said Jerry.

'You here?' said Henry.

'Just going,' said Jerry, and an observer, eyeing him as he made for the door, would have felt that if he was not grinding his teeth, he, the observer, did not know a ground tooth when he saw one.

It was some hours later, when up in the clouds on his journey back to London, that he suddenly remembered that he had omitted to collect Biff's Boudin.

3

Biff was annoyed and in his opinion justifiably annoyed. He was not, he said, an unreasonable man, he did not demand perfection and could make allowances when necessary, but he did feel that when a fellow sent a fellow over to Paris to get a picture for him, the fellow was entitled to expect the fellow to come back with the damned thing. Instead of which, he went about the place leaving it behind. Was that, he asked, the way to win friends and influence people?

Jerry put up the best defence he could.

'I did mention it to Kay, I told her about it directly I arrived. But we got talking of other things, and then Blake-Somerset came in, and he made me so mad that I just rushed out.'

'Forgetting the picture?'

'It never entered my mind.'

'Such as it is. Why did he make you mad?'

Jerry did not speak for a moment. He was trying to cope with the rising feeling of nausea which the recollection of that revolting scene in the living-room of 16 Rue Jacob never failed to induce. When he did speak, his voice quivered.

'He kissed her!'

This puzzled Biff.

'Very natural, surely? It's the first thing you do when you're engaged to a girl, or even when you aren't, for that matter. Good Lord!' said Biff, as a curious gulping sound proceeded from Jerry's lips. 'Are you telling me you've gone and fallen in love with Kay?'

Jerry would have preferred not to be obliged to confide in one whom he knew to be of a ribald turn of mind, but it seemed unavoidable. Curtly he replied that he had, and Biff was surprisingly sympathetic.

'I don't wonder. Even a brother's eye can see that she has what it takes. She's always been very popular. There was a nouveau art sculptor in Paris who said he was going to shoot himself if she wouldn't marry him. He didn't, which was a pity, because obviously the more art nouveau sculptors who shoot themselves, the sweeter a place the world becomes. Well, well, so that's how it is, is it?'

'Yes, it is. Any objections?'

'None whatever. No harm in it at all, as far as I can see. You may be the beneficent influence which will divert her fatheaded little mind from that frozen fish of hers. I think with perseverance you may swing it, for I can't believe she seriously intends to marry that human *bombe surprise*. Shall I tell you something, Jerry? It's just a theory, but I believe the reason Kay teamed up with Henry Blake-Somerset was that he was so different from all the other men she knew. When a girl has been mixing for two years with the sort of blots who made up the personnel of our Parisian circle and somebody comes along who hasn't a beard and dresses well and looks as if he took a bath every morning instead of only at Christmas and on his birthday, something she may easily mistake for love awakes in her heart. But it can't last. Given the will to win, you should be able to cut him out. Have you taken any steps?'

'I told her I loved her.'

'What did she say to that?'

'She reminded me that she was engaged to Henry Blake-Somerset.'

'And then?'

'That's all.'

'You mean you left it at that?'

'What else could I do?'

Biff was concerned. There came into his manner a suggestion of a father rebuking a loved but erring son.

'You'll have to show more spirit than this, Jerry o' man. You seem to have conducted your wooing like a cross between a scared rabbit and a jellyfish. That's not the way to win a girl's heart. You ought to have grabbed her and kissed her and gone on kissing her till she threw in her hand and agreed to play ball.'

'We were talking on the telephone.'

'Oh? I see. Yes, that would be an obstacle. And I suppose

you couldn't have done it when you saw her this last time because Blake-Somerset was present, which would naturally have cramped your style. But bear in mind for your future guidance that what I have outlined is the procedure if you want to get anywhere. I've tested it a hundred times. Meanwhile let me say that I am no longer incensed because you forgot to bring the picture. It was an outstanding boner, but if it was love that made you pull it, I can readily understand and forgive, because for your private files, Jerry, I, too, love. I told you about Linda Rome, didn't I?'

'You said you were once engaged.'

'And we're now engaged again. I've bought the licence, notified the registrar, who requires a day's notice, and the wedding will take place shortly.'

Jerry was not one of those self-centred young men who, having troubles of their own, are incapable of rejoicing in a friend's good fortune.

'Well, that's splendid. Congratulations. How did you find her?'

'Oh, very fit, thanks. A bit aloof for a moment or two, but it soon wore off.'

'I mean, when last heard from you were trying to get her address. Did you get it from Tilbury's secretary?'

'Er – no. No, she didn't give it to me. I happened to run into Linda in Bond Street, where the picture galleries are. I'd gone there with the idea of finding out the current prices of Boudins. It seems she now works for one Gish, who peddles paintings for a living, and she was emerging from his joint just as I was going in and we collided on the doorstep.'

'Embarrassing?'

'Not after the first moment or two. Everything went like a breeze. I said "Hello, Linda" and she said "Well, I'll be damned if it isn't Biff" or words to that effect, and after we'd kidded back and forth for awhile I took her off to the Bollinger bar, where we shared a half-bot and fixed everything up. Time, the great healer, had done its stuff and we were sweethearts still. She told me the reason I hadn't been able to locate her was that she had given up her apartment

84

and was living with Tilbury out at Wimbledon. He has one of those big houses on the Common.'

'So I've heard. Didn't the secretary tell you she was living there?'

'No. No, she didn't mention that.'

'Odd. She must have known. But she isn't an intelligent girl.'

'You know her?'

'Not to speak to. I've seen her around. A strikingly beautiful blonde. I was only going by her appearance when I said she wasn't intelligent. Most blondes aren't.'

At an early point in the proceedings Biff had mixed himself a refreshing drink and had been sipping it slowly as they talked. He now drained what was left in his glass with a gulp, and a gravity came into his manner.

'There's something you can do for me, Jerry. There's a little favour I'm asking of you, which will cost you nothing but will be of a great help in stabilizing my position with Linda.'

'I thought you said it was stabilized.'

'To a certain extent, yes, but only to a certain extent.'

'So—?'

'So I should be infinitely obliged if, when you meet Linda as of course you will ere long, you don't bring the conversation around to Gwendoline Gibbs.'

'I ought to be able to manage that, seeing that I've never heard of her in my life. Who is Gwendoline Gibbs?'

'Tilbury's secretary.'

'Oh, I see. The fellow who pointed her out to me didn't tell me her name. You don't want me to mention her?'

'If you would be so kind. I don't mind telling you that though Linda has consented to go registrar's-office-ing with me, I'm still, as you might say, on appro. She admits to loving me, but gives the impression that she does it against her better judgement. The least suspicion that I am still the trailing arbutus I used to be, and that registrar will lose a fee. As I think I told you, it was my gentlemanly preference for blondes that led her to sever relations a year ago, and between ourselves, Jerry, in the couple of days before I ran into her on Gish's threshold I was giving Gwendoline a rather impressive rush. So if, when conversing with Linda, you find yourself running short of small talk, speak to her of the weather, the crops and any good books she may have read lately, but don't fall back on Gwendoline Gibbs. On the subject of Gwendoline Gibbs let your lips be sealed.'

'I'll see to it.'

'That's my boy. It will ease the situation greatly. Extraordinary how complex life has become these days, is it not? What with Gwendoline Gibbses and Spendthrift Trusts ... By the way, Tilbury has heard about the will. The New York lawyers, the ones who wrote the letter that followed, told him. Linda happened to be in his office and found him putting in a transatlantic call to them, all agog to get the low-down. She describes him as turning a rich magenta and uttering animal cries when they broke the bad news, and I'm not surprised. One can well imagine that the information would have given him food for thought. The next time she saw him he told her he was going to contest the will on the ground that the late Pyke was cuckoo. You don't think he can swing that, do you?'

'I don't see how. From what you've told me, Mr Pyke had his eccentricities, but nothing more than that, and after all he was your godfather.'

'And he had neither chick nor child, which was a bit of luck for the chicks and children, as I remember him.'

'He probably looked on you as a son. Kay tells me you saved his life once, and apparently he wasn't fond of Tilbury, so why shouldn't he leave you his money?'

'You're a clear thinker, Jerry. I've always said so.'

'And Tilbury can't plead undue influence. Generally when someone brings a suit of that kind, it's because it has come out that the heavy wrote a will leaving everything to him and got the testator to sign it on his death bed, guiding his hand as he used the pen. Obviously there can't have been anything like that in this case, because you haven't seen your godfather for three years. You can't influence people by remote control.'

Biff drew a relieved breath.

'What a comfort you are, Jerry. It's an odd thing. Anybody looking at you would say you were just an ordinary sort of dimwit, whereas in reality you have this colossal brain and this extraordinary grasp of legal minutiae. You aren't a lawyer in disguise, by any chance, are you?'

'I read law at Cambridge but I never ate my dinners.'

'What was the trouble? Weak stomach? No appetite?'

Jerry explained that in order to become a member of the English bar the young aspirant is obliged to consume a number of evening meals at the Hall of his Inn or Court, and Biff said he had never heard anything so loopy in his life. It confirmed, he said, the impression he had already formed that everybody connected with the Law, except possibly Perry Mason, should be certified.

'What happens if you're a vegetarian?'

'I suppose you pass up the plat du jour and fill in with potatoes and cheese. I can't tell you for certain because, as I say, I never tried it. But getting back to what we were talking about I don't think you need worry.'

Biff was silent for a moment.

'There is one thing that worries me a little, Jerry o' man, due, I suppose, to that mellowed feeling of wanting to be a do-gooder which I believe I mentioned to you. We can't deny that I owe my present prosperity entirely to old Tilbury.'

'I don't get that.'

'Obvious, surely. If he hadn't been such a stinker, Pyke would have left him the whole bundle. By being a stinker he became the founder of my fortunes, and I think he ought to have his cut. I believe I'll slip him a piece of change.'

'Very generous.'

'Well, I want smiling faces about me. I'll rout out a solicitor and have him draw up an agreement whereby in exchange for waiving all claim to the lettuce Tilbury receives five per cent of the gross. Would your uncle do that for me? Then I'll go and see him directly I'm dressed. Lincoln's Inn Fields he hangs out in, I think you told me.'

CHAPTER SIX

In supposing that his telephone conversation with Mr Leonard Haskell of the legal firm of Haskell and Green would have given Lord Tilbury food for thought, Biff had not erred. The letter which he found on his desk two days later gave him more. In the course of their transatlantic exchanges Mr Haskell had spoken of a letter already on its way to him by air mail. It contained, said Mr Haskell, full particulars of the late Mr Pyke's last will and testament and should reach him at any moment now. And here, as promised, it was.

Lord Tilbury's initial emotion on opening it and learning of the Spendthrift Trust was a heartening feeling that things were looking up. He had consulted his solicitor in the matter of contesting the will on the ground that Mr Pyke had been incompetent to make one, and his solicitor had not been encouraging, reasoning that it was very unlikely that a man capable of salting away ten or so millions of dollars could have been of weak intellect. But this letter, with its careful exposition of the conditions of the Spendthrift Trust, put new heart into him and showed him that all was not lost.

He knew Biff and was familiar with his record. Surely, he felt, unless the young wastrel had undergone a complete change of character, it should be a mere matter of days before the arm of the law gripped him on some pretext or other. According to Mr Haskell's letter, unless he had totally misread it, arrest for even so trivial an offence as being drunk and disorderly would be enough to rule Edmund Biffen Christopher out. And if Edmund Biffen, exhilarated by the thought of his glittering prospects, did not become drunk and disorderly at the earliest opportunity, Lord Tilbury felt that he would lose his faith in human nature.

Only when the chilling reflection came to him that Biff,

with so much at stake, probably would have undergone a complete, if temporary, change of character did his optimism wane. Reason told him that at current prices for good behaviour even the most irresponsible of young men would certainly keep his feet glued to the straight and narrow path.

Unless – and here optimism returned – he were assisted off it by outside sources. That, he saw, was an avenue that he would do well to explore. Was there not some way by which this promising young disturber of the peace could be induced to get back to normal and start disturbing it again?

Motionless at his desk, ignoring the letters he should have been dictating to Gwendoline Gibbs and ceasing for the moment even to think of Gwendoline Gibbs, Lord Tilbury gave the full force of his powerful intellect to the problem, spurred on by that urge which makes all very rich men eager to add to their riches.

For perhaps twenty minutes nothing stirred, and then suddenly something shook him like an electric shock. The thought of Percy Pilbeam had flashed into his mind, and his reaction was somewhat similar to that of a war horse hearing the sound of a bugle.

Pilbeam! If there was one man in existence capable of employing the conditions of the Spendthrift Trust to the undoing of Biff, it was Percy Pilbeam. He had always had the deepest respect for his former underling's ingenuity and unscrupulousness, and he knew that if adequately paid no-one would be more likely to see to it that the conditions of the Spendthrift Trust produced practical results. What steps Percy Pilbeam, having pouched his fee, would take he could not say, but there was no doubt in his mind that they would be steps of impressive, if fishy, brilliance.

He decided to seek him out that afternoon as soon as his duties at Tilbury House would permit. The idea of inviting him to dinner at his club he dismissed. He was a man rather acutely alive to class distinctions and he felt that Percy, liberally pimpled and favouring the sort of clothes that made him look like a Neapolitan ice cream, would not do him credit at his club. Better to call and see him at his business address.

This was not far from Barribault's Hotel, for the Argus Enquiry Agency, which had started in a modest way in a single room in the Soho neighbourhood, had long since moved to Mayfair and had enlarged itself to an ante-room and two inner rooms. One of these, the smaller, was occupied by a couple of stenographers: in the other, in a leather chair which in the early days would have been far beyond his means, Percy Pilbeam sat waiting to receive clients. The ante-room was in the charge of a gentlemanly office boy.

It was to the last-named that Lord Tilbury handed his card, and the boy looked properly impressed as he took it into his employer.

'Someone to see me?' asked Percy Pilbeam, glancing up from the papers which were engaging his attention.

'A *lord* to see you, sir,' said the office boy. A polished lad, he loved the aristocracy.

Percy inspected the card, shocked the boy by saying 'Oh, old Tilbury? All right, send him in,' and sat back in his leather chair, well pleased. He always enjoyed meeting this former employer of his, for the sight of him brought back the days, now long past, when, like Ben Bolt's Alice, he had wept with delight when he gave him a smile and trembled with fear at his frown. Not that Percy had ever quite done that, for even when on the pay roll of the Mammoth Publishing Company he had always had far too good an opinion of himself to be servile, but he had certainly gone in awe of Lord Tilbury at that period of his career and now he did not. To him his erstwhile boss was just another client, and he wondered what he had come about.

It was not immediately that Lord Tilbury put him in possession of the facts, for he seemed oddly reluctant to state his business. He said the weather was fine, which it was. He said these were nice offices, which they were. He said that he had never ceased to regret the day when Percy had severed his connection with Tilbury House, which was true, adding that since Percy's departure he had not been able to find a satisfactory editor for *Society Spice*. It was left for Percy to get down to what are commonly called brass tacks.

'Something you wanted to see me about, Tilbury?'

'Well, – er – yes, Pilbeam. The fact is, I find myself in a somewhat delicate position.'

Percy Pilbeam had started his career at Tilbury House as assistant editor of *Pyke's Home Companion*, in which capacity – under the pseudonym of Aunt Ysobel – it had been his duty to conduct the Answers To Correspondents page, giving advice to the lovelorn each week, and for an instant, as Lord Tilbury, obviously embarrassed, made this confession, he found himself speculating as to whether the other was approaching him now in his Aunt Ysobel role and was about to confide in him with regard to his love for Gwendoline Gibbs. Should this be so, he was quite ready to oblige. If Lord Tilbury wanted to know if it would be a welcome or an unforgiveable act to press Gwendoline's hand he was amply equipped to inform him. If Lord Tilbury had come to enquire if it would help things along if he were to kiss Gwendoline on the forehead, he could supply the answer. He waited confidently for him to proceed.

When, however, Lord Tilbury did proceed, it was along quite unexpected lines.

'Pilbeam,' he said, 'I had a brother named Edmund.' and it occurred to Percy to wonder if by any possibility this old employer of his had been lunching injudiciously.

'He died recently.'

As far as was possible for a man with pimples, sideburns and a small black moustache to look sympathetic, Percy did so. A few graceful words to the effect that he felt for Lord Tilbury in his bereavement floated into his mind, but he left them unspoken, as he did a rather neat line about all flesh being as grass. He did not want to delay whatever it might be that was coming next.

'He settled in America as a young man,' said Lord Tilbury, becoming quite fluent, 'and did extraordinarily well. Towards the end of his career he was one of New York's leading financiers, and as the greater part of his fortune was made before the days of high income taxes, he was at the time of his death extremely rich. I do not think I am exaggerating when I say that his estate must amount to at least ten million dollars.'

Anything to do with money, particularly money running into the millions, enchained Percy's interest.

'Coo!' he said, and whistled. 'Who gets it?'

'That is precisely what I came here to talk to you about, Pilbeam. Naturally, as his only surviving relative except for a niece whom he had never met, I expected to inherit, but I do not.'

'What happened? Did he leave it all to charities?'

'No.'

'Is there a widow?'

'No.'

'Then why don't you collect?'

'Don't ask me!' said Lord Tilbury. 'I think he must have been insane. He made a will leaving everything he possessed to a godson of his. I get nothing.'

His hard luck story did not really fill Percy with pity and terror, for, like Linda Rome, he considered that his visitor was quite rich enough already, but he tried to infuse sympathy into his voice.

'That's tough. But where do I come in? Why did you want to see me?'

Lord Tilbury's initial embarrassment had vanished. He had come to the offices of the Argus Enquiry Agency to seek aid in a scheme which even he could see fell under the heading of dirty work at the crossroads, and for awhile he had been reluctant to put it into words. But there was something about Percy Pilbeam, as he sat curling his moustache with a pen, which made it easy to confide the rawest and most dubious propositions to him. You felt that he would understand and sympathize.

'I am hoping that you will be able to help me. Have you ever heard of a Spendthrift Trust?'

Percy said he had not.

'It is the general term, the New York lawyers tell me, applied to Trusts which the beneficiary cannot dispose of in advance. I have never heard of them myself, but apparently they are quite usual in the United States, and in some states, such as New York, all trusts have this characteristic. Yes, yes, I am coming to the point,' said Lord Tilbury, for Percy had suggested that he should. 'The point is this. Some Spendthrift Trusts further provide that if the beneficiary shall commit some act or behave in some manner of which the testator does not approve, he forfeits his rights and the money goes to another beneficiary. It was this that my brother specified in his will. If his godson, a young man named Christopher, is arrested for any misdemeanour before his thirtieth birthday, he forfeits everything and the money comes to me as the next of kin. I beg your pardon?'

Percy Pilbeam had not spoken except to say 'Ouch!' His companion's words had caused him to start so abruptly that the pen with which he was curling his moustache had slipped and inflicted a nasty flesh wound on his upper lip.

'Christopher, did you say?'

'Yes.'

'Is his name Biff?'

'I believe his friends call him that. He was christened Edmund Biffen after my brother.'

'Well, what a coincidence!'

'You know him?'

'I was out with him only the other night. I happened to meet him with a girl I know.'

He phrased the remark discreetly. It would have been foreign to his policy to reveal to his visitor that the girl who had won his heart was the cousin of anyone so low in the social scale as a private investigator. Lord Tilbury, he knew, admired his brain and lack of scruple, but that did not mean that he would welcome him as a member of his family. Time enough to tell him after the wedding.

'He kept saying he was a millionaire, but I thought he had come into a little money and just *felt* like a millionaire. He took me on a pub crawl. You should have seen him put the stuff away.'

'He drank heavily?'

'I'll say he did.'

'How very satisfactory,' said Lord Tilbury, beaming.

'Then you are the man to help me. I knew I was not making a mistake in coming to you, my dear Pilbeam.'

'But why me?'

It was a little difficult for Lord Tilbury to explain this without hurting anybody's feelings. As we have seen, what had given him the idea of placing his affairs in the hands of the proprietor of the Argus Enquiry Agency had been the recollection that in the old *Society Spice* days Percy had shown himself eager and willing to undertake any questionable work that came his way. Indeed, if it did not come his way, he had gone out and looked for it. Subsequent editors of *Society Spice* had been inclined to draw the line somewhere – Jerry Shoesmith was a case in point – but Percy Pilbeam had been above this weakness. The sky, where he was concerned, had always been the limit.

'Because I have such confidence in your brains and ingenuity, Pilbeam. I thought that you might somehow make this young Christopher's acquaintance and – er – well, you see what I had in mind. And now I find that you already know him. Things could not be more satisfactory.'

He had no need to enlarge on his point. Percy Pilbeam might wear sideburns and a Neapolitan ice cream suit, but he was quick at the uptake.

'I see what you mean. You want me to have another night out with the fellow and get him tight.'

'Exactly.'

'So that he'll do something to make him get pinched by the police and lose the money according to the terms of the Trust and you'll collar the whole ten million.'

'You put these things so clearly, Pilbeam. That is just what I want you to do.'

'And what,' said Percy, 'is there in it for me?'

Lord Tilbury, knowing his Pilbeam, had anticipated that this query would be coming, and he had steeled himself to meet it. He never enjoyed paying out money, but he knew that if you do not speculate, you cannot accumulate.

'A hundred pounds.'

'Or, rather,' said Percy, 'a thousand.'

Lord Tilbury was seated at the moment, so he did not

sway and totter, but his jaw fell and his eyes protruded like Biff's at the sight of a blonde. He gasped.

'A thousand!'

'An insignificant percentage on what you will be getting.'

'Two hundred, Pilbeam.'

'A thousand.'

'Five hundred.'

'A thousand was what I said. No, on second thoughts, make it two thousand.'

Lord Tilbury breathed heavily. His face had taken on the purple tinge of which Linda Rome had spoken. He looked like a toad which was not only beneath a harrow but suffering from high blood pressure. But gradually the purple flush faded. The healing thought had come to him that as this conversation was taking place without witnesses present, he could always later on repudiate any promises to which he might bind himself. It was surely unlikely that Pilbeam would do anything so crude as to insist on a written agreement.

'Very well,' he said.

'You agree?'

'I do.'

'Then we'll just have a little written agreement,' said Percy. He took up the pen with which he had fondled his moustache and wrote rapidly on a pad. He rang a bell, and the gentlemanly office boy entered. 'Oh, Spenser,' he said, 'tell Lana and Marlene to come here.'

The two stenographers made their appearance, witnessed the document and withdrew. They were both attractive young women, but Lord Tilbury, as he watched them append their signatures, thought he had never seen two more repulsive members of their sex. But it is to be doubted if even Gwendoline Gibbs would have seemed attractive to him, had she been rendering legal a document which was going to reduce his bank balance by two thousand pounds.

'And now,' said Percy, 'I'll tell you what I'm going to do. I'm going to get hold of Joe Murphy.'

'I beg your pardon?'

'And introduce Christopher to him. Murphy is a man I

know in Fleet Street who has the most astonishing capacity for absorbing alcoholic liquor. He's famous for it. Nobody can have an evening with Joe and not feel the effects. And we know what happens to Christopher when he has a few drinks. He wanted to wind up our night out by punching a policeman.'

'And you restrained him!'

'Well, how was I to know? But it'll be all right this time. After he's met Murphy he's bound to end up punching someone. I can't guarantee a policeman, of course.'

'No, no.'

'Still, even a civilian will do the trick.'

'Quite.'

'So there we are.'

'So there we are,' echoed Lord Tilbury.

The expression 'It's in the bag' was not familiar to him, or he would certainly have used it.

2

The morning following the Tilbury-Pilbeam conference found Biff in tender and sentimental mood. He and Jerry were sitting over the remains of breakfast, and he was telling Jerry, who was trying to read his paper, how deep was his love for Linda Rome. It was a subject on which he had touched a good deal since his arrival at Halsey Chambers.

'But it's odd,' he said.

'What's odd?'

'The whole set-up,' said Biff. 'Why do I have this extraordinary urge to marry Linda and accept no substitute? The dullest eye can see that it's a thoroughly unsuitable match, and my best friends would try to draw me back from the abyss. "Don't do it, Biff," they'd say. "Be advised while it is not too late. The mate for you is some merry little soul who gets tight and dances on supper tables." But I don't want any merry little souls, I want Linda and nobody but Linda. How do you account for that?'

'You're getting some sense at last.'

'That may be it. Of course, she's an angel in human form and will bring out the best in me. But I sometimes wish her ideals were not so high.'

'You think she'll take some living up to?'

'Quite a bit. Not that I blame her. She has her reasons. Did I ever tell you she'd been married before? Guy called Charlie Rome on the Stock Exchange. He drank like a fish and was always chasing girls.'

Jerry wrinkled his forehead.

'Now who does that remind me of? Someone I've met somewhere. No, it's gone. What did she do? Divorce him?'

'Yes. She stuck it as long as she could, and then called it a day and no doubt felt much easier. But the reason I bring Charlie Rome up is that her experience with him has given her extremely rigid views on the subject of behaviour in the male sex. It has led her to stepping up her matrimonial requirements.'

'The next in line has got to be someone in or around the Sir Galahad class?'

'Or he hasn't a hope. You see, then, what the future holds for me. I shall have to reform myself from the bottom up, do all the things I don't want to do, be respectable, settle down, limit myself to a single cocktail before dinner and one glass of wine during it. Under her gentle guidance I shall grow a double chin, bulge at the waistline till none of my pants fit me, become a blameless stuffed shirt and probably end up as a Congressman. But do I shudder? Have I qualms? No, I like it. I look forward to it. With Linda at my side, I know it'll be worth the discomfort.'

'In fact, you're purified by a good woman's love.'

'A very neat way of putting it.'

'You want to be worthy of her trust.'

'Exactly. That's why it's such agony to think how I have deceived her.'

'When did you deceive her?'

'Well, I haven't yet, but I'm going to this morning. I'm giving Gwendoline Gibbs lunch today, and one of Linda's wishes, as I think I told you, is that I shall steer clear of blondes. She made me promise I'd never speak to a blonde again, and you can't sit there and say that Gwendoline Gibbs doesn't fall into that category.'

'What on earth are you giving her lunch for? Why don't you cancel the date?'

'Impossible. You can't just drop a girl like a hot coal. You've got to taper off. This is a farewell lunch, and one of the things causing me concern is that I'm not by any means sure I've enough money to pay for it. I'm running very short. I shall be all right, of course, directly Kay brings that picture. Linda tells me a Boudin's worth all sorts of money. You said she was expecting to be able to get over here yesterday. Well, where is she? I see no signs of her.'

'If she came yesterday, it was probably fairly late and she would be busy getting settled in a hotel.'

'She could have phoned. She could have relieved my suspense and anxiety by putting in a simple inexpensive telephone call saying that everything was under control. Well, why didn't she?'

'Didn't think of it, I suppose.'

'Exactly. Couldn't be bothered. To hell with a brother's nervous system. Let him eat aspirin. I'll tell you something about Kay which may make you think twice before leading her to the altar, Jerry o' man. She's thoughtless. She doesn't put herself in the other fellow's place. She knows I'm in imminent danger of dying of malnutrition unless she takes the lead out of her pants and gets a move on with that picture, she knows it's my only source of income and without it I shall soon be reduced to stealing the cat's milk and nosing about in ash cans for crusts of bread, but she delays, she dallies, she loiters, she ... Ha!' said Biff as the telephone rang in the hall. 'That may be the wench now. Go and hear what she has to say. And don't waste precious time telling her you love her, get the facts.'

Some minutes elapsed before Jerry returned from his mission. Biff eyed him eagerly.

'Was it Kay?'

'Yes, it was Kay all right. She couldn't come yesterday. She's arriving tonight.'

Biff heaved a sigh of relief.

'Excellent. The sun breaks through the clouds. That means I shall have that Boudin tomorrow.'

'It would,' said Jerry, correcting this view, 'if she were bringing it. But she isn't.'

'What! Not bringing it? Don't I get any service and co-operation? Why isn't she bringing it?'

'She told me to tell you you were better without it. She thinks it would be fatal for you to have a lot of money.'

Biff reeled. His were serviceable ears, ears in which hitherto he had had every confidence, but he was looking now as if he could not believe them.

'She said that?'

'She did.'

'My own sister! A girl whom I have watched over for years with a brotherly eye.'

'And now she's watching over you with a sisterly eye,' said Jerry unsympathetically. 'Surely even you can see she's quite right. You know what you're like. You can't afford to get into trouble at this stage of the proceedings, and you'd certainly do it if you had the necessary funds. You ought to be applauding her sturdy commonsense.'

The telephone rang once more. This time it was Biff who went to the door.

'I'll get it. If that's Kay again,' he said grimly, 'I'll tell her what I think of her sturdy commonsense. She'll think the receiver in her hand has jumped up and snapped at her.'

He strode out, a cold and haughty figure. When he came back, his drawn face had relaxed and was illuminated by a happy smile. He looked like a man whose faith in his guardian angel has been restored.

'It was Pilbeam,' he said. 'You remember Pilbeam?'

'I do.'

'Nice guy, don't you think?'

'I do not. The original human rat.'

Biff clicked his tongue disapprovingly, but more in sorrow than in anger.

'Try to correct this jaundiced outlook, Jerry. He's nothing of the sort. He's the salt of the earth – pimpled, yes, but full to the gills of outstanding merits, and if you want to know how I know, I'll tell you. He's asked me to look in on him this afternoon and says he can put me in the way of making a bit of money. That's the sort of man Percy Pilbeam is.'

A chill wave of horror swept over Jerry. His was a really vivid imagination, and he could picture what this would mean.

'Don't touch it!' he cried. 'Think what you'll be losing.'

'I don't follow you.'

'You know what'll happen if you get hold of money. You'll go whooping it up and getting pinched.'

'Absurd. Don't you think I have any sense?'

'No.'

'You're wrong. I'm bursting with it. However, I've no time to go into that now. I'm meeting Gwendoline at the Berkeley at one and I have to make my toilet. I should be glad, by the way, if you would lend me a trifle. In order to finance the farewell lunch I shall need at least three pounds, though if you think five's safer, I shall raise no objections. So let's have them, Jerry o' man, and then Ho for the open road.'

3

There are few trysts an impecunious young man keeps with more meticulous punctuality than those which hold out the promise of cash changing hands, and Biff was not a moment late for his appointment at the Argus Enquiry Agency. Percy in their telephone conversation had asked him to be there at three, and it lacked but a minute to the hour when he strode blithely into the ante-room and requested the office boy Spenser to inform the big shot that Edmund Biffen Christopher was at his service. Like a flash he found himself in Percy's presence, the honoured guest, and Percy was clasping his hand and offering him a cigar and urging him to take a chair and make himself comfortable. He could scarcely have had a more impressive reception if the Argus

Enquiry Agency had laid down a red carpet for him and loosed off a twenty-gun salute.

Both host and guest had lunched well and were in excellent fettle, and this caused the proceedings to be conducted from the start in that atmosphere of the utmost cordiality in which statesmen are always basking at round table conferences. It was only after compliments had been exchanged, healths enquired into and the weather briefly discussed that Percy struck the business note.

'You told me on the telephone this morning,' he said, 'that you would like to make a bit of money,' and Biff replied that a bit of money was the very thing he was wholeheartedly in favour of making. As Percy was aware, he went on to add, his prospects could be described as rosy – or glittering, if Percy preferred that word – but he was at the moment sorely in need of ready cash. The smallest contribution, he said, would be gratefully received.

'You suggested on the phone that you had a job for me.'

'I have.'

'Something in the private ocular line?'

'I beg your pardon?'

'Detective work, is it?'

'You could call it that.'

'Oh?' said Biff, and fingered his chin a little dubiously. He was reluctant to cast a damper on this extraordinarily pleasant chat, but he felt it was only fair to issue a warning. 'Well, I wouldn't want you to go into this thing with your eyes shut, so I ought to tell you at the outset that I'm not what you'd call versed in the sleuthing art. I don't suppose I'd recognize a clue if you brought it to me on a salver with full explanatory notes attached. So if you're expecting me to measure bloodstains and analyse cigar ash and find out where someone was on the night of June the fifteenth, you're in for a disappointment. Was it something along those lines that you had in mind?'

As a rule during business conferences Percy Pilbeam took pains to preserve an impassive gravity, holding quite correctly that it made a better impression, but there were occasions when, not being aware how repulsive it made him look, he permitted himself a smile. He did so now.

'No, no, nothing of that sort. The job I'm thinking of doesn't call for technical skill.'

'Good,' said Biff, 'because, as I was telling you, technical skill is just what I'm short of. I imagine private-eye-ing is one of those things where you've either got the knack or you haven't. Like roller skating or riding a bicycle.'

'Quite. But I'm not asking you to do anything very difficult.'

'What *are* you asking me to do?'

Before replying, Percy rose from his chair, tiptoed to the door, flung it open, satisfied himself that Spenser the office boy was not leaning on it with a gentlemanly ear glued to the keyhole and returned to his desk. Biff followed him with an interested eye, feeling that this was the stuff.

'Top secret?' he queried, impressed.

Percy gave a brief nod which, like Lord Burleigh's, spoke volumes.

'Very much so. I assume I can rely on your complete discretion?'

'Oh, sure.'

'Because this is strictly between ourselves ... and, of course, Scotland Yard.'

'Scotland Yard, eh?'

'They have called me in. They often do when there is some special work to be done.'

'You don't say!'

'The Yard has its limitations. For certain types of crime – murder, arson, burglary and so forth – their machinery serves them well enough, but when it comes to a delicate matter of this sort, no. I'm sure you agree with me?'

'I probably would if I knew what the hell you were talking about. You haven't told me what the delicate matter is.'

'Oh, haven't I? Well, it doesn't need much explanation. I want you to make the acquaintance of a man named Murphy. It's no use Scotland Yard trying to get at him, he would spot a Yard man a mile off. But he would never suspect you. You are so obviously what you make yourself out to be, a young American going about London seeing the sights and having a good time. I'm sure you'll be able to fool him.'

'I'll do my best, than which no man can do more. Why do you want me to fool him? Who is this child of unmarried parents?'

Percy put a finger to his lips and sank his voice to a whisper.

'Open that door.'

'Which door?'

'That door.'

'Oh, that door?'

Biff obligingly opened the door and stood awaiting further instructions, but Percy, apparently satisfied, waved him back to his seat.

'I thought Spenser might be listening,' he explained, and once more Biff was impressed by these precautions. He was beginning to feel that he was in the secret service and would shortly have to be prepared to find himself addressed as X-1503. 'Who is this man, you were saying. Murphy, as he calls himself, though his real name is probably something ending in ski or vitch, poses as a freelance journalist, one of those fellows who drift about Fleet Street picking up jobs, but we know that he's an agent of a certain unfriendly power—'

'Which shall be nameless?'

'No names, no pack drill.'

'I'll bet it's Russia.'

'Very smart of you to guess it.'

'Your saying his name ended with ski or vitch gave me the clue.'

'Quite. Well, the Yard wants to find out what he's up to. There's something cooking – they know that – but the question is what, and that's where you come in. He's always at The Rose and Crown in Fleet Street at night. I'll introduce you – I know him fairly well – and then you can sit down with him and become friendly—'

'And find out what he's up to?'

'Exactly.'

Biff was silent for a moment.

'May I raise a point?' he said. 'One would perhaps describe this Murphy roughly as an international spy, I take it?'

'Exactly.'

'Well, aren't international spies inclined to be on the cagey side? That's how they always are in the books I've read. Don't think I'm trying to make difficulties, but isn't there just a chance that he'll maintain a cold reserve and refrain from sobbing out his secrets on my shoulder? It's worth considering.'

Once more, Percy permitted himself that smile of his which was so like something out of a horror film.

'I was coming to that. You will of course see that he drinks heavily and loses his caution.'

'But that means I'll have to drink, too.'

'Of course. If you're thinking of the expense, that will be taken care of. Before you leave this office, I will give you ten pounds. Call again tomorrow, and you will find another forty waiting for you, and if you manage to extract anything from this man, anything of value that will give Scotland Yard something to go on, it will be looked on as money well spent.'

He paused, and a deep sigh escaped Biff. It sounded like the rustling of bank notes receding into the distance. He was remembering his promise to Linda Rome to confine himself to a single cocktail before dinner and a single glass of wine during the meal and at other times to exercise an austerity as rigid as that of Gwendoline Gibb's Uncle Willie, the notorious total abstainer. He was at a loss to see how this ascetic régime could be combined with tying on a bundle with international spies in Fleet Street pubs.

And yet ... fifty quid ... at a time when he had never needed a financial shot in the arm more. ...

He wavered.

And then Linda's face rose before his eyes, and he was strong again.

'I'm sorry –' he began, and was on the point of making the great renunciation when the telephone rang.

'For you,' said Percy Pilbeam, handing him the instrument.

'Biff?' said the telephone.

'Oh, hello, Jerry.'

'Listen, Biff,' said Jerry, and his voice was urgent. 'I've got some disturbing news, I'm afraid. Your Linda Rome rang up a moment ago.'

'Ah yes. Wanting to speak to me, of course.'

'She thought she *was* speaking to you, for she started right off, not giving me a chance to say who I was, by stating that she had seen you lunching with a blonde –'

'Death and despair!'

'And when there was a lull, which wasn't immediately, and I said I wasn't you, she said Oh, wasn't I and wanted to know where she could get in touch with you. I told her you'd gone to the Argus Enquiry Agency, and I imagine she'll be giving you a buzz shortly.'

'Despair and death!'

'So I thought I'd better give you this word of warning, so that you'd have time to knock together a story of some kind. Think quick, is my advice, for I can assure you that her voice was frosty. She spoke like a girl who wanted an explanation, and a fairly full one. Well, goodbye and best of luck.'

'Bad news?' said Percy Pilbeam, as he replaced the receiver. 'For you,' he added a moment later, as the instrument rang again.

This time, beyond an 'Oh, hello, honey' sheepishly spoken by Biff, all the talking was done at the further end of the wire. It was plain to Percy Pilbeam that whoever was doing it was of the female sex, which is celebrated, when on the telephone, for never allowing the party of the second part to get a word in edgeways. He noted the slow drooping of his companion's jaw and the look of dismay that came into his eyes. An able diagnostician, he had no difficulty in deducing that Biff was being properly told off by some unseen lady friend, and if he had had a heart, it would have probably bled for him. He, too, had been told off by lady friends in his time.

But business was business, and he was glad when at last – after shouting 'But, listen, Linda! Listen! Listen!' – Biff returned the receiver to its place.

'Well, how about it?' he said. 'Will you take the job?'

Biff seemed to wake from a trance. He blinked like a boxer who has injudiciously placed the tip of his nose in the orbit of an adversary's glove. He looked at Percy as if weighing up his qualifications as a confidant, then seemed to decide that a man who wore a small black moustache and was curling it with a pen was not the proper recipient for the story of his lost love. A stern, determined expression came into his face, the look of one whose heart has been cracked in several places, but who sees the way, now that it is no longer necessary for him to humour a woman's whims, to getting his hands on a substantial sum of money. Bring on your international spies, he might have been saying, and I will drink Scotch for Scotch with them. Or bourbon, for that matter. Or rye.

'Sure,' he said, 'I'll take it,' and he strode from the room, a sombre, dignified figure who would have reminded a more widely read man than Percy Pilbeam of Shelley's Alastor, and Percy resumed his work, well content. He was skimming through some photostats of letters which would eventually enable Mrs F. G. Bostock of Green Street, London WI to sever her matrimonial relations with Mr Bostock, when a thought struck him. He reached for the telephone and called Tilbury House, asking for the office of its proprietor.

'Gwen?'

'Oh, hullo, Perce.'

'Listen, Gwen, are you seeing anything of that fellow Christopher these days?'

'Quite a lot. We've just had lunch together. Why?'

'Well, give him a miss.'

'But he's a millionaire.'

'He's not a millionaire, and he's never going to be one.'

'What do you mean?'

'Listen,' said Percy.

It had not been his intention to reveal to any outside party the business arrangement into which he had entered with Lord Tilbury, for he considered that these things are better kept in strict confidence between principal and agent, but it had not taken him long to recognize that here was a special case. In language adapted to the meanest intelligence, and there were few meaner intelligences than that of his cousin Gwendoline, he unfolded every detail of that business arrangement, omitting nothing.

'So don't you have anything more to do with the fellow,' he concluded. 'You wait for Tilbury.'

'Coo!' said Gwendoline. 'I'm glad you told me.'

CHAPTER SEVEN

I T was with a pensive look on her face that Kay, having established herself overnight at a modest hotel in the Bloomsbury neighbourhood, rang the bell of Number Three Halsey Chambers, on the following morning. She was thinking of Henry Blake-Somerset and more particularly of his mother, relict of the late Sir Hubert Blake-Somerset of Lower Barnatoland and The Cedars, Mafeking Road, Cheltenham.

The lunch to meet Henry's mother had been an uncomfortable meal. It is only very rarely that there can exist a perfect fusion of soul between the widow of a British colonial governor, accustomed to associate with Service people in a town like Cheltenham, and a girl who is not only American – always a suspicious thing to be – but who lives in Paris – of all cities the one with the most dubious reputation – and is probably a bohemian with loose friends who drink absinthe and play guitars in studios. To Lady Blake-Somerset, who had been brought up on *Trilby*, no girl living in Paris could possibly have the smallest claim to respectability, and Kay's charm, which so powerfully affected Jerry Shoesmith, had spent itself on her in vain. Her attitude, in short, had resembled that of the mother in the old music hall song who, introduced to her son's fiancée, looked at her meditatively and said 'Poor John! Poor John!' Lady Blake-Somerset had not actually used the words 'Poor Henry!' but her manner throughout lunch had implied them, and Kay, thinking of her now, frowned thoughtfully.

Her frown vanished as the door opened and she saw Jerry. Once again she had that sudden lift of the heart at the sight of him. It gave her the feeling of having come home where she would be understood and appreciated.

'Hello there,' she said. 'Well, here I am. Why the glassy stare? Weren't you expecting me?'

Jerry had been staring glassily because, as always, there

was something about her that affected him like a blow on the base of the skull with a blunt instrument. He recovered himself with an effort, but was not immediately capable of speech.

'I'll go away if you like,' said Kay.

'For God's sake don't say things like that,' said Jerry with a shudder. 'Welcome to Meadowsweet Hall. What do you think of it?'

'Cosy,' said Kay, coming in and looking about her. 'I'd have thought an establishment run by a couple of bachelors like you and Biff would have been a shambles, but it looks fine. Where is our Biff, by the way?'

'Still asleep, I imagine. His door's shut.'

'Lazy young devil.'

'And lucky for you he *is* asleep.'

'Why so, professor?'

'Because if he saw you before he's had time to calm down, he would probably put a brother's curse on you, and brother's curses are not to be sneezed at. He was very emotional when I told him about the picture.'

'Don't you think I was right not to bring it?'

'Of course you were. How much was that picture worth?'

'About ten thousand dollars.'

'Can you envisage Biff making the rounds with all that in his hip pocket?'

'My flesh creeps.'

'So does mine.'

'Gosh, I wish it was you and not Biff who had to keep out of trouble. You're the sober, steady type.'

'What a revolting thing to say of anyone.'

'Meant as a compliment. If you knew the dregs of the underworld Biff has collected around him in Paris, you'd understand. He's so amiable that he can't bring himself to choke off the scrubbiest deadbeat who wants to make friends. He comes in and lays them on the mat with a cheery "Meet old Jules or old Gaston" or whoever it may be, and once they're in the woodwork you can't get them out. Honestly, I don't believe I know a single soul in Paris who isn't a freak of some kind, except my colleagues on the

Herald-Trib. And Henry, of course.' She broke off abruptly, her eyes round and horrified. 'Oh, heavens!' she cried. 'Oh, my fur and whiskers!'

'What's the matter?'

'I've just remembered I was supposed to be lunching with Henry today.'

A chill fell on Jerry's mood of happiness. He had been looking forward to a cosy lunch with her himself, and while he knew that these disappointments are good for the character, strengthening it, he was unable to enjoy this one. He spoke a little coldly.

'Well, why the agitation? You've plenty of time. He's in London then?'

'No, in Paris, where he thinks I am. I didn't tell him I was coming here. I was to have lunched at Prunier's with him and his mother.'

'He has a mother, has he?'

'And how!'

'You speak as if you didn't like her much.'

'I don't, and she doesn't like me.'

'She must be crazy.'

'But what am I to do? How shall I explain?'

'Oh, tell him you walked in your sleep or got amnesia or something. Why explain at all?'

'But he'll be furious.'

'I doubt it. Coldly annoyed, perhaps, but not furious.'

'Well, anyway,' said Kay, cheering up in the mercurial way habitual with her, 'there's nothing to be done about it now. Let's talk about you. I was surprised to find you at home at this hour of the morning. The Sergeant told the Commissaire's secretary that you described yourself as an editor. Well, why aren't you editing?'

'I've been fired.'

'Oh, I'm sorry.'

'I'm not. It was a loathsome little rag.'

'Who fired you?'

'My Lord Tilbury.'

'I've heard about him from Biff. He's Linda Rome's uncle.'

'He's also the boss of the Mammoth Publishing Company, which owns *Society Spice*, which I edited. He didn't like the way I was doing it, so he dispensed with my services.'

'Well, I hope he breaks a leg. Oh!'

'Now what?'

'I've just thought what to tell Henry. I'll say the paper sent me over to London about something without warning, and I hadn't time to let him know.'

'It sounds thin to me.'

'To me, too, on reflection, and I'm afraid it'll sound thin to Henry. He'll be chilly.'

'Isn't he always? Are you familiar with the poems of Robert W. Service?'

'Not very.'

'He wrote about the Yukon.'

'I knew that much.'

'He stresses that the air there has quite a nip to it. Frost, snow and ice abound, and the man who hasn't his winter woollies is out of luck. I've often thought the Yukon would be Henry Blake-Somerset's spiritual home.'

Kay regarded him thoughtfully.

'Shall I tell you something?'

'I'm always glad to hear from you.'

'I don't believe you're really fond of Henry.'

'Not very, though I might be if I were an Eskimo.'

'They think a lot of him at the Embassy.'

'How do you know that?'

'He told me so. He'll probably be an ambassador some day.'

'Thus making a third world war inevitable. Don't talk to me about Henry. He's a pill to end all pills.'

'Don't forget that he very kindly put you up for the night in his pill box.'

'And I wrote him a bread and butter letter, thanking him. A charming letter it was, too, considering that his hospitality nearly gave me pneumonia.'

'No hot water bottle?'

'Hot water bottles didn't enter into it. It was my host who chilled me to the marrow. The man's as cold a fish as I ever encountered off a fishmonger's slab, and how you can contemplate marrying him is a mystery to me. He'll be one of those stiff, starchy husbands, breaking your heart with that Embassy manner of his. I shudder at the picture of your home life which my imagination is conjuring up. It'll be like living in a refrigerator. Henry Blake-Somerset has all the charm and warmth of a body that has been in the water several days with the thermometer in the low twenties.'

'Mr Zoosmeet, you are speaking of the man I love!'

'Bah!'

'What did you say?'

'I said Bah.'

'Well, don't say it again.'

'I shall say it every time you talk clotted nonsense about loving that stuffy, supercilious, glassy-eyed walking corpse.'

'That'll make you entertaining company.'

'More entertaining than Henry.'

'Will you stop picking on Henry?'

'No, I will not. Nothing shall prevent me speaking my mind fearlessly on the subject of that sub-zero drip.'

Kay sighed.

'Our first quarrel! You're being a bit bossy, aren't you, Zoosmeet? Throwing your weight about somewhat, it seems to me. If I wasn't so refined, I'd toss my curls at you. Not that it isn't very civil of you to be so concerned about me.'

'You're the only thing in the world that matters to me, and I simply refuse to accept this delirious stuff about you marrying somebody else. You're going to marry me. Good Lord, can't you see that we were made for each other? You can't have forgotten those days on the boat. We were twin souls. And you babble about marrying Henry Blake-Somerset! One hardly knows whether to laugh or weep. But thank heaven I'm in time to avert the disaster. I have the situation well in hand. Do you know what Biff was saying to me yesterday?'

'Something crazy, I'll bet.'

'Not at all. He gave me the soundest advice. There was solid sense in his every word.'

'Then it can't have been Biff, it must have been a couple of other fellows.'

'He told me the way to cure you of this absurd Henry obsession of yours was to grab you and kiss you and keep on kissing you till you got some sense into your fat little head. And that is precisely what I propose to do here and now, so get set.'

'Would you lay your hand upon a woman?'

'You bet I would. Both hands. I'll show you who's a sober, steady type,' said Jerry, and as he spoke there came a loud and insistent ringing from the front door.

'Saved by the bell!' said Kay. 'I've always heard that Heaven protected the working girl. Who would that be, do you think? Lord Tilbury come to say he's sorry he was cross and you can have your job again?'

It was not Lord Tilbury. It was Biff. He tottered into the room, his aspect so closely resembling that of the water-logged corpse to which Jerry had recently compared Henry Blake-Somerset that simultaneous gasps of horror proceeded from both his sister and his friend. They had no words.

Nor had Biff many.

'Lost my key,' he said. 'Oh, hello, Kay. Well, good night, all,' he added, and sinking into a chair went to sleep.

2

Kay gazed dumbly at Jerry. Jerry gazed dumbly at Kay. The same thought was in both their minds, that this poor piece of human wreckage, so like a beachcomber in a Somerset Maugham short story or the hero of a modern play, must have been on the bender of a lifetime. Even Jerry, who had known him in his New York days when he was at his sprightliest and most uninhibited, was awed. When he spoke, it was in a hushed whisper.

'Golly!'

'Golly is correct.'

'Angels and ministers of grace defend us! Are you seeing what I see?'

'I am.'

'We'd better get him to bed.'

'And keep him there.'

'And while you're tucking him in and telling him his bedtime story, I'll be going out and buying bicarbonate of soda. It'll probably only scratch the surface, but it may help.'

Kay shrugged her shoulders.

'Get it if you like, but he won't need it. That's what's so maddening about Biff, he has these orgies and they don't do a thing to him. He wakes up as fresh as a daisy and starts planning new excesses with a song on his lips. I think it must be something to do with the glands.'

Jerry was amazed. By some chance, when in New York, he had never happened to see Biff on the morning after.

'As fresh as a *daisy*?' he said incredulously, eyeing the remains in the chair. 'You mean no hangover? No remorse? No ice on the head? No vows of repentance? No suggestion that he's off the stuff for life?'

'None. It breaks my heart. If only he'd suffer as he deserves to, I'd be able to bear it, but he doesn't. It makes you feel there's no justice in the world. Still, toddle along on your errand of mercy, if you want to.'

When Jerry returned, Biff had disappeared, presumably into his bedroom, and Kay was sitting in the chair he had occupied, on her face the look which made Walter Pater say of another of her sex that this was the head upon which all the ends of the world were come. It wrung his heart to see her.

'Cheer up,' he said, gently consolatory. 'I know how you're feeling, but you mustn't let it get you down. Naturally this has given you a shock. No sister likes to see a loved brother looking as if he had been celebrating Hogmanay in Glasgow. I wouldn't myself, if I were a sister. But things aren't as bad as they might have been. After all, he's back in the fold and not in a prison cell. Everything's all right, it seems to me.'

His bedside manner failed to exercise a soothing effect. Kay gave no indication of sharing his sunny outlook. Anybody wishing to know the difference between an optimist and a pessimist would only have had to glance at the two of them to inform himself.

'I'm glad you think so,' she said. 'I wish I could. What happens when he cuts loose again? His luck can't hold for ever.'

'He mustn't be allowed to cut loose again.'

'How are you going to stop him? I wish there was some way of keeping him in the fold, as you put it, and never letting him go out.'

'There is. I'll pinch his trousers.'

'What!'

'These simple methods are always the best. His pantaloons, I'll abstract them. That'll stabilize him.'

Kay was silent for a moment.

'It's a thought,' she agreed. 'But won't he bide his time and get hold of a pair of yours?'

'I shan't be here. I shall go and plant myself on my Uncle John, who lives at Putney. He won't like it, nor shall I, but that can't be helped. I can stand Uncle John for a day or two, and he'll damned well have to stand me. It only requires resolution. Here's the set-up, as I see it. I move out of here, you move in. I take Biff's garments to Putney, you go back to your hotel and pack. I meet you there and escort you to lunch at Previtali's in Oxford Street,' said Jerry, naming one of London's smaller and less expensive restaurants. 'And over the meal I shall have much to say to you on the subject we were discussing just now. Any questions?'

'None. You seem to have covered everything.'

'I think so.'

'How is Biff off for trousers?'

'He has only two pairs. No Beau Brummel he. He tells me he had to skip out of Paris in what he stood up in and on arrival in London purchased a spare at a secondhand clothing establishment. You'll have no difficulty in gleaning the full harvest. I think you had better be the one to do it. You tread more softly than I do. Can you sneak into his room without waking him?'

'I imagine nothing will wake him for hours.'

'Then let's get cracking. Why are you looking at me like that?'

'I was just drinking you in, wondering if you were always as brilliant as this.'

'Nearly always.'

'I also wondered why you were grinning like a Cheshire cat.'

'You noticed the slight smile? I was thinking of Henry and what a jolt he's going to get when he fetches up at Prunier's with his mother and finds you aren't there. I wouldn't be surprised if he didn't raise his eyebrows.'

3

But all Henry Blake-Somerset's eyebrow-raising had been done on the previous evening, when, his mother having decided that she preferred Maxim's to Prunier's, he had telephoned Kay at the *Herald-Tribune* office to let her know of the change of venue and had been informed that she had already left for London.

His eyebrows then had certainly shot up, and he had come as near to using intemperate language as a member of an Embassy staff ever does, for the news had confirmed his worst suspicions. He could think of but one reason why Kay should have left for London. She must have made an assignation with the man Shoesmith. He remembered the night when she had come with Shoesmith to his apartment, the two of them patently on terms of camaraderie as cordial as those of a couple of sailors on shore leave. He remembered Shoesmith's thin story of how he and she had met by pure chance that evening at a police station, not having seen each other for two years. He remembered Shoesmith's furtive telephone call. And he had not forgotten finding Shoesmith with Kay at her apartment that day when he had come to take her to lunch to meet his mother.

It was, he felt, an intolerable state of affairs and one that called for decisive action on his part. He must confront her, and confront her without an instant's delay. It was his intention, in short, to talk to her like a Dutch uncle.

And so, having notified the Embassy authorities that he would be unable to be with them that day owing to a severe attack of neuralgia, he had hastened to Orly after his coffee and marmalade and taken the first plane leaving for England.

Like Othello, Henry Blake-Somerset was perplexed in the extreme.

CHAPTER EIGHT

LORD TILBURY, as was his habit, had got to his desk shortly before ten that morning, but he did not, as he usually did, proceed to concentrate steadily on the work before him. He found himself unable to keep his mind on it. He dictated one or two letters to Gwendoline Gibbs, then dismissed her to the outer office and sat drumming his fingers on the blotting pad. He was waiting tensely to hear from Percy Pilbeam and learn what had happened to Biff on the previous night.

After what seemed a lifetime the telephone rang.

'Tilbury?'

'Lord Tilbury speaking,' said Lord Tilbury shortly and with perhaps undue emphasis on the first word. Much as he admired Percy's brains and lack of scruple, he found the air of chummy equality he assumed these days more than a little trying. He sometimes felt that the time was rapidly approaching when his former employee would call him George. 'Yes, Pilbeam, yes? Have you news for me?'

'It was a flop,' said Percy. He did not believe in wasting breath by trying to break things gently. 'Something must have gone wrong, and I can't understand it. I've got Murphy with me now, and he tells me Christopher was cockeyed when he left him, but I've just rung Halsey Chambers and he answered the phone, so he must have got home all right. I'd have betted anything he'd have finished up at a police station,' said Percy with the sombre gloom of a man who has failed to add two thousand pounds to his bank account, than which there is none more sombre, except of course that of the man who has failed to add ten millions.

Lord Tilbury, falling as he did into the latter class, was shaken to the core. It was not for some considerable time after Percy, with a moody 'Well, there it is', had hung up the receiver that he achieved anything approaching calm, and when he did, his mind could not have been described as tranquil. He felt low and dispirited, in sore need of something to raise him from the depths, and, as men in that condition so often do, he yearned for a woman's soothing companionship. He had not intended to go to the length of asking Gwendoline Gibbs to lunch until his courtship had progressed somewhat further, but he recognized that this was an emergency. He rose from his chair and opened the door of the outer office.

'Oh, Miss Gibbs.'

'Yes, Lord Tilbury?'

'I was ... er ... it occurred to me ... I was wondering if you would care to join me at luncheon?'

Gwendoline's beautiful face lit up, encouraging him greatly, but a moment later it fell.

'Oh, Lord Tilbury, I should love to, but have you forgotten that you asked Mr Llewellyn to lunch today?'

If there had not been ladies present, Lord Tilbury would probably have done what old-fashioned novels used to describe as rapping out an oath. The appointment had passed completely from his mind.

'He said today is the only day he can manage, as he is flying to Rome tomorrow. He is calling for you here at one-thirty.'

The day was warm, but Lord Tilbury found himself shivering. The thought of Ivor Llewellyn of the Superba-Llewellyn motion picture corporation calling at Tilbury House and finding that his host had walked out on him without a word of explanation was a chilling one. No proprietor of a morning paper, an evening paper, a Sunday paper and four film magazines can afford to offend the president of a large Hollywood studio with thousands of pounds of advertising at his disposal. And Ivor Llewellyn, he knew, was a touchy man.

'Thank you, Miss Gibbs,' he said gratefully. 'Thank you for reminding me. Some other time, then, eh?'

'Oh, yes, Lord Tilbury.'

'I forgot to ask you how you were feeling today? You had a slight headache yesterday. Quite gone, I hope?'

'Oh yes, Lord Tilbury.'

'And how is Champion Silverboon of Burrowsdene?'

'*Who?*' asked Gwendoline blankly. She searched her mind, such as it was. 'Oh, you mean *Towser.*'

'Towser?'

'I call him Towser. The other name was so long.'

'Of course. Yes, quite. Very sensible.'

Back in his office, Lord Tilbury, though regretting that he would share the mid-day meal with a motion picture magnate who always bored him a good deal and not with the goddess of his dreams, was elated rather than depressed. He felt he had made progress with his wooing. He had given this girl flowers, chocolates and a Boxer dog which he rather wished she had not decided to call Towser, and now he had invited her to lunch. Short of actually asking her to be his, there was, he considered, nothing much more a man could have done.

He was musing thus and wishing the telephone would ring and that it would be Mr Llewellyn informing him that having just slipped a disc he regretted, like Miss Otis, that he would be unable to lunch today, when the telephone did ring.

The caller, however, was not Ivor Llewellyn, whose discs were in mid-season form and who in his room at the Savoy was at this moment taking a bath in order to be fresh and sweet for the Tilbury luncheon, it was Percy Pilbeam again, and he seemed excited.

'Tilbury?'

'Lord Tilbury speaking.'

'I've been talking to Murphy, Tilbury. He's just left me.'

Lord Tilbury said 'Oh?' and there was a wealth of indifference in the word. The mysterious Murphy had ceased to be of value to him and he could not have cared less about his comings and goings.

'And do you know what he said? He said he had been talking to an American newspaper chap, and this newspaper chap had told him that your brother was as loony as a coot. Did you ever think of contesting the will on the ground that he wasn't competent to make one?'

'It was naturally the first idea that occurred to me. I consulted my solicitor, but he was discouraging. He said I had no evidence.'

'Well, you will have when you've heard what Murphy's friend told Murphy.'

Until this moment Lord Tilbury's voice had been cold. There was something about Percy Pilbeam on the telephone that always jarred him, a breezy familiarity that filled him with the conviction that Percy Pilbeam was getting above himself and needed taking down a peg or two. But at these words he ceased to think hard thoughts of him, being now of the opinion that he was a splendid young fellow deserving of nothing but the highest esteem. He burned with remorse that he had ever even mentally criticized this admirable private investigator.

'Yes, Pilbeam? Yes? Go on, Pilbeam.'

'What did you say, Tilbury? Speak up. Don't mumble.'

'What did Murphy's friend tell him?'

'His name's Billingsley.'

'Never mind his name.'

'And he's on *Time* or *Newsweek* or one of those papers. His editor told him to go and interview your brother, so he wrote asking if he could make an appointment, and your brother wrote back naming a day. His letter was written in red chalk.'

'In what?'

'Red chalk. Each word outlined in blue chalk. Like Hyman Kaplan.'

'I beg your pardon?'

'Let it go. He asked Billingsley to lunch, and when he got there he told him they were going to lunch backwards.'

Once more Lord Tilbury begged his young friend's pardon. The statement had bewildered him.

'He said it was an experiment he had often wanted to try, because he thought so many lunchers get into a rut. They began with coffee and cigars and worked back through a glass of port, chocolate soufflé and breaded veal cutlet with potatoes and asparagus, finishing up with aperitifs and Martini cocktails. Billingsley said it was quite an experience. And after lunch, when he tried to interview the old bird – sorry, your late brother – all the old loony – your late brother, I mean – would do was play records on the gramophone and tell Billingsley to shut up when he tried to say anything. He just sat there sipping his third cocktail and tucking into the potted shrimps and playing records. He was particularly fond of Dorothy Shay. He played that Mountain Girl song of hers sixteen times and was still playing it when Billingsley left.'

The receiver shook in Lord Tilbury's hand. He had been hopeful, but he had never expected anything as promising as this.

'Good gracious, Pilbeam! That story told to a jury –'

'Exactly. That's just what I'm driving at. And there's something else. Over the breaded veal cutlets your brother began talking of Charles Fort and saying that he was a disciple of his.'

'Who is Charles Fort?'

'Was, you mean. He's dead. I haven't time to tell you about him now, but you have reference books in your office. Look him up. Well, there you are, Tilbury old man. Go and spring your evidence on Christopher and watch him wilt. His address is Three, Halsey Chambers, Halsey Court.'

Lord Tilbury drew a deep breath.

'I will go and see him immediately,' he said.

2

Returning from Putney after depositing his suitcase with its precious freight and looking in at Halsey Chambers to see how Biff was coming along, Jerry was amazed by the spectacle that met his eyes. Kay's prediction that her brother would emerge from his coma as fresh as a daisy he had been regarding as mere poetic imagery, but a glance was enough to tell him that she had in no way exaggerated. Except for a spectacular black eye, there was plainly nothing wrong with their wandering boy. Only a very up and coming daisy could have been in better shape. He was wearing pyjamas and a dressing gown, and he greeted Jerry with a heartiness which could not have been exceeded by the most confirmed teetotaller. He might have been drinking lemonade for a life-time, like Percy Pilbeam's father.

'Hello, Jerry o' man,' he cried buoyantly. 'I couldn't think what had become of you. Where you been?'

'I went to Putney.'

'The name is new to me. Where's Putney?'

'It's a riverside suburb. My uncle lives there. I'm going to stay with him for a few days. Kay's moving in here. She wants to be on the spot to watch over you. She thinks you need a woman's care.'

Biff laughed indulgently.

'These girls! Always fussing.'

'Well, you can't say your appearance this morning wasn't enough to cause alarm and despondency. I came here to make sure you were still alive.'

'You caught me just in time. I was on the point of going out.'

'You were, were you?'

'To see Linda and heal the breach.'

'So there was a breach? I thought there might be when she was speaking to me on the phone. Did she get you at the Argus?'

'She did, and she said quite a number of things that wounded my sensitive nature more than somewhat. I think I spoke to you once of her tendency, when stirred, to be-have like a charge of high explosive. The general impres-sion I received from her remarks was that the betrothal was off and that if I cared to jump in a lake with a pound of lead in each hand, it would be all right with her. But don't worry, o' man. Shed no tears. I can fix things up. I have the infal-lible system. You remember what I recommended in the case of you and Kay, the close-embrace-and-kiss routine? Did it work, by the way?'

'I didn't have a chance to try it. You interrupted us.'

'Too bad. I should have timed my entry better.'

'Incidentally, how did you come to be in such a state?'

'Couldn't be avoided. I'd been having a night out with an international spy.'

'Biff, you're still tight!'

'Not a bit of it. Percy Pilbeam arranged the thing. That was what he called up about. Certain parties not unconnected with Scotland Yard asked him to get hold of someone to go and ply this spy with drink in order to learn his secrets, and Percy wanted me to take on the job. I was about to turn down his offer, because I'd promised Linda to lay off the sauce, but then her call came through and I no longer considered that I was bound by my promise, so I accepted the commission, strongly influenced by the fact that there was a hundred and forty dollars at the current rate of exchange in it for me.'

'For doing what?'

'I told you. Revelling with this spy. I can't tell you anything more, because the men up top would be annoyed if I spilled the details. We fellows who work for the Yard have to be discreet. Just leave it at this, that the international bimbo and I split a wassail bowl at the Rose and Crown in Fleet Street and it overheated me a good deal, though it had no apparent effect whatever on the cloak and dagger boy. I'll tell you something that'll be helpful to you in your career, Jerry o' man. Never get drinking with international spies, because they have hollow legs. This one finished the evening as sober as a new-born babe, as far as I could ascertain. I admit that in the later stages of our reunion I was seeing him through a sort of mist, but he looked unruffled to me. Guy who calls himself Murphy, though it's widely known at Scotland Yard that his real name's Ivanovitch or Molotov or something. Nice fellow. Collects stamps.'

'Did he give you that black eye?'

'Good Lord, no, ours was a beautiful friendship throughout. I told him all about Linda's extraordinary behaviour, and he told me all about these stamps of his. The black eye came much later, when I was on my way home and entering Halsey Court. I can't tell you exactly what happened, but I do remember having a hell of a fight with someone, or a group of citizens it may have been. It's all a bit vague. You know how it is when you've been hobnobbing with international spies, your memory gets blurred.'

At the thought of what could so easily have happened Jerry's heart congealed.

'You might have been arrested!'

'The same thought occurred to me later. Very fortunate that I wasn't. One feels that there is a Providence that watches over the good man. But we were talking of how I proposed to effect a reconciliation between Linda and self. I shall steer her into some unfrequented spot and kiss her soundly and all will be forgiven.'

'You think so?'

'I'm sure of it. What makes you dubious?'

'I was thinking of her attitude when she was speaking to me on the phone.'

'Oh, that? Pay no attention to that. Girls never mean half what they say when with receiver in hand. The instrument goes to their heads and they just babble on with the first thing that occurs to them. She's probably shedding bitter tears of remorse at this very moment. And now, if you'll excuse me, Jerry o' man, I'll be going and dressing and getting about my business. Nothing could be more delightful than sitting chatting with an old friend like you, but –'

He broke off. The telephone had rung. He rose and went out into the hall with a fond 'I shouldn't wonder if this wasn't Linda now.'

'Hello?' he said. 'Yes, speaking ... *Who?* ... Why, sure, if you want to ... Where are you? Barribault's? Then you'll be able to get here quick, which is very desirable because I shall have to be going out soon. All right, then, I'll be expecting you. That was old Tilbury,' he said, coming back to Jerry. 'He says he wants to have a talk with me, one presumes about the testamentary dispositions of the late Edmund Biffen Pyke. I can't think of any other topic we have in common.'

'Do you want me to go?'

'Don't dream of it.'

'Shan't I be in the way?'

'On the contrary, you will lend me moral support. Does he know you by sight?'

'I shouldn't think so. We've certainly never met. Editors

of *Society Spice* don't mix much with the big chief. Of course he may have seen me somewhere.'

'Immaterial. He won't remember you. Yours is one of those ordinary, meaningless faces that make no impression on the beholder. Then you will figure in the coming interview as my solicitor, here to watch over my interests. When he arrives, put the tips of your fingers together and sniff a good deal. If he calls me names, look legal and talk about defamation of character before witnesses. Should he become violent, kick him in the slats. Ha,' said Biff, as the bell rang. 'This, if I mistake it not, Watson, is our client now.'

It was indeed Lord Tilbury whose thumb had pressed the button and was now, for he was in impatient mood, pressing it again. He was looking forward with the utmost confidence to the coming interview. Years of intimidating obsequious underlings had left him with a solid belief in his power to bend others to his will, particularly if they were mere popinjays like this young Christopher. He was convinced that it would not be long before Biff wilted beneath the eye which had caused so many of his age group to wilt. There was something very formidable in his aspect as he entered the room. If he had been carrying a placard with the words 'Take to the hills, men, here comes the first Baron Tilbury,' it might have added to the impressiveness of his demeanour, but not much.

'Good morning,' he said menacingly.

'Good morning,' said Biff. Then, seeing that his visitor was directing an enquiring eye at Jerry, he added 'My solicitor, Mr Henderson of Henderson, Henderson, Henderson, Henderson and Henderson. The year the firm started,' he explained, 'happened to be a bumper year for Hendersons. Quite a glut of them there was. You could scarcely give them away. Well, come in, Tilbury o' man, and take the weight off your feet. What can I offer you in the way of refreshment?'

Lord Tilbury frowned.

'This is not a social call.'

'Business?'

'Precisely.'

'Stand by, Mr Henderson.'

'I'm here,' said Jerry.

Lord Tilbury breathed heavily. His acquaintance with Biff was slight, but he had always disliked him and never more than at this moment. Nor was there anything about the young wastrel's legal adviser that appealed to him. As far as possible, he decided to ignore the man.

'I will begin by saying,' he said, addressing himself to Biff, 'that I have been in communication with my brother's lawyers in New York.'

'And how were they?'

'They informed me of the terms of his will. I have come to discuss them.'

'And you couldn't have picked a better time. Mr Henderson and I were just discussing those terms ourselves. What's biting you? Something in that will you didn't like?'

'I intend to contest it and have it set aside.'

'Forget it, Tilbury. You won't get to first base. How do you feel about it, Mr Henderson?'

Jerry put the tips of his fingers together.

'On what grounds, Lord Tilbury, do you propose to contest the will?'

'On the ground that my brother was mentally incompetent to make one.'

'If mentally incompetent means what I think it means,' said Biff, 'you haven't a hope. What interpretation do you place on the words "mentally incompetent", Mr Henderson?'

'They would suggest that in Lord Tilbury's opinion the late Mr Pyke was –'

'Loony?'

'Bonkers.'

'That is the legal term, is it? Thank you, Mr Henderson. And put those damned fingertips of yours together,' said Biff in an undertone, for Jerry had relaxed his vigilance in this respect. 'I don't say,' he went on, 'that Edmund Biffen Pyke wasn't peculiar in some ways, but he was sane all right. Not a gibber in him.'

'I have evidence to submit.'

'Let's have it.'

'He wrote letters – serious business letters – in red chalk. And he lunched backwards.'

'I don't get that.'

Lord Tilbury gave a brief description of the entertainment offered to Mr Billingsley of *Time*, or it may have been *Newsweek*, and Biff dismissed the episode with a careless wave of the hand.

'I don't think much of that. Anything further?'

'Yes. He was a disciple of Charles Fort.'

'Charles who?'

'Charles Fort.'

'Never heard of him. You ever hear of Charles Fort, Mr Henderson?'

'He was an American writer. Wrote several books.'

'You see. These solicitors know everything. How does he get into the act? Why does Pop Tilbury say "He was a disciple of Charles Fort" in that meaning way, as if he'd caught us with our pants down?'

'Well, his views were considered rather odd. He believed that the sky is a solid mass of some jellied substance and that the stars are holes where the light shines through. He used to warn flyers to watch out for this jelly and avoid it.'

'Very sensible. Might have given themselves a nasty knock.'

'He also believed that mysterious disappearances like those of Judge Crater and Dorothy Arnold were caused by their being snatched up by unseen forces who live in this jelly. Just an idea, of course, but it did lead to some people thinking him eccentric.'

Lord Tilbury's snort might well have been mistaken for the Last Trump.

'Eccentric! He was as mad as a hatter, and my brother was the same.'

'What do you think, Mr Henderson?'

Jerry's fingers were pressed together as if with glue, and his sniff was that of a man who knew his Coke and Littleton backwards.

'I disagree. Eccentricity is not madness. Charles Fort had quite an impressive following. When the jury hears that among his disciples were men like Alexander Woollcott and Theodore Dreiser, it will be difficult to persuade them that, simply because Mr Pyke also believed in his theories, he was mentally incompetent to will his money however he pleased.'

'Well spoken, Mr Henderson, and you can tell all the other Hendersons I said so. What do you say to that, Tilbury, o' man? Cooks your goose to some extent, does it not? Or don't you think so?'

Lord Tilbury did not.

'I see that it is useless to continue this conversation further,' he said. 'I shall merely say that I am prepared to make a concession in order to avoid litigation.'

'Which is?'

'These things are always better settled out of court. If you are agreeable to dividing the money equally between us, I shall be satisfied. Failing that, I propose to contest this will if I have to take the case to the Supreme Court of the United States. I will leave you to think it over. Good morning, gentlemen,' said Lord Tilbury, and he stalked out, a dignified figure.

3

In the room he had left the prevailing atmosphere was one of sober triumph. It was Biff's opinion that they had fought the good fight and given the forces of darkness something to think about in their spare time. He was particularly effusive on the subject of the part played by his solicitor Mr Henderson.

'You were superb, Jerry o' man. I don't know what I'd have done without you at my side. I'm fairly intrepid, but I might quite easily have quailed before old Tilbury's wrath, had I been called upon to face it alone. He's a tough guy. When I was engaged to Linda, she took me once or twice to dine at his Wimbledon residence, and he never failed to intimidate me. I guess you have to be pretty formidable to run a business like his. I take it, by the way, that you were right in thinking he won't get anywhere with that contesting-the-will suit he was sounding off about?'

Jerry was reassuring.

'I'm fairly sure he won't. He couldn't win his case on evidence like that. You haven't a thing to worry about except the Spendthrift Trust.'

'Which causes me no anxiety whatsoever.'

'Nor me ... now.'

'You think we've got it licked?'

'I'm sure we have.'

Biff beamed.

'It's great to know that you've such faith in me, Jerry. I thought perhaps after last night you might have been entertaining doubts. I did betray your trust a little last night. It won't occur again.'

'I know it won't.'

'Thank you, Jerry o' man, thank you. You don't know what your confidence means to me. I shall now go out and contact Linda with a light heart,' said Biff, making blithely for his bedroom.

It was perhaps three minutes later that he appeared again. When he did, his face wore a puzzled expression. He looked like a dachshund trying to remember where it has buried its bone.

'Most extraordinary thing, Jerry o' man. I can't find my pants.'

'Your pants? Oh, yes, your pants. I forgot to tell you about that. I took them to Putney.'

'You ... *what?*'

'Kay was a little worried as to what you might get up to if you had them, so I suggested removing them and she thought it an admirable idea. We agreed that we would both be much easier in our minds if we knew you were safe and snug at Halsey Chambers and not running loose about London. You'll get them back on your birthday. Nice birthday present.'

'But I've got to go and see Linda!'

'She'll still be there when you rejoin the human herd.'

It was plain from Biff's face that he was running what is

called the gamut of the emotions. A stunned disbelief seemed for awhile to predominate, but it soon yielded to righteous indignation. Owing to his overnight misadventures he had only one eye to glare with, but he made it do the work of two.

'And you call yourself a pal!' he said bitterly.

'The best you ever had, my lad, as you'll realize when you think it over in a calm, reasonable spirit. I'm saving you from yourself, and if you care to look on me as your guardian angel, go right ahead. Not that I want any thanks.'

'You damned well won't get them.'

'I thought I mightn't. Well, I must be off. I'm picking Kay up and taking her to lunch. Any message I can give her?'

For some moments Biff spoke forcefully. In spite of Jerry's assertion that the initiative in this foul conspiracy had been his, he was convinced that the brains behind it had been Kay's and that Jerry had been a mere instrument or tool. He expressed himself on the subject of Kay as no brother should have expressed himself about a sister.

'I see,' said Jerry, nodding. 'Just your love.'

4

The door closed behind Jerry, and Biff stood for some moments as motionless as if he had been posing for an artist anxious to transfer to canvas a portrait of a young man of dachshund aspect clad in a dressing gown and disfigured by a black eye. A wave of self-pity poured over him, and it would not have taken much to make him break down and sob. It was so vital that he should seek Linda out and talk her into a more amenable frame of mind before her present animosity solidified beyond repair.

And then there floated into his mind the thought of the Brothers Cohen, and out of the night that covered him, black as the pit from pole to pole, there shone a ray of hope, like the lights of a village inn seen after long wandering by a wayworn hiker.

The Brothers Cohen, as everybody knows, conduct their

secondhand clothing emporium in the neighbourhood of Covent Garden, and it is their boast that they can at a moment's notice supply anyone with any type of garment his fancy may dictate. Their establishment is a Mecca for all who unexpectedly find themselves caught short sartorially, whether they be African explorers down to their last solar topi, Government officials in the Far East in need of new cummerbunds or merely diners-out requiring instant dinner jackets. Biff's first act on reaching London after leaving Paris without stopping to pack had been to go to them and make a few additions to his wardrobe, and now the memory of that visit came back to him and with it the complacent feeling that those who had plotted against his person were going to be made to look pretty silly. His thoughts, as he went to the telephone and dialled the Cohen number, might have been condensed into the familiar phrase 'You can't keep a good man down.'

The Cohen Brothers were charming. They booked his order with as much enthusiasm as if it had been the first they had had for months. If pants were what he required and if he would supply them with his waist measurement, they said, pants should be at his address just as soon as their Mr Scarborough could get there in a taxi cab. And it was in an incredibly short time that he heard the bell ring and leaping to the front door found a beautifully dressed young man with a large parcel standing on the mat.

'Mr Christopher?'

'That's right.'

'My name is Scarborough.'

'I was expecting you,' said Biff. 'Come right in, Scarborough o' man, and if you'd care for a quick one, you'll find the makings in the closet over there.'

A good many dukes and earls drop in on the Cohen brothers when they need ermine-fringed robes to wear at the opening of Parliament or raiment suitable for the royal enclosure at Ascot, and some of the polish of these aristocratic clients rubs off on the staff of attendants. So much had rubbed off on their Mr Scarborough that he might have been the son of a marquis in good standing or of a particularly respectable baronet. He was a blond young man with a small moustache which would have interested Percy Pilbeam, that moustache aficionado, and his diction was pure B.B.C.

'Nothing to drink for me, thank you very much,' he said in a voice of which even an announcer of the Fat Stock Prices would not have been ashamed. 'We at headquarters feel ourselves bound by the same restrictions as policemen when on duty. Nothing in the nature of definite orders, of course, simply an unwritten rule which we all obey. Sort of tradition, you know. You are the gentleman requiring pants?'

Biff said he was, and might have added that the desire for pants of all other gentlemen desiring pants was tepid compared with his.

'I have them here. Your order gave rise to a little indecision at headquarters, for you did not specify the type of pants you required. We have the long in flannel, the short in flannel, the long in linen, the short in linen and also summer zephyrs in meshknit. As the weather is so warm, it was assumed that you would prefer the knee-length meshknit.'

Biff's one eye was riveted on the contents of the parcel, and an observer would have noted in it bewilderment, frustration and chagrin. It is disconcerting to ask for bread and be given a stone, and it is equally disconcerting to find that your plea for trousers has been answered with knee-length meshknit underlinen.

'What on earth are those things?' he demanded.

Mr Scarborough said they were pants, and Biff uttered a snort of a calibre which put him in the Tilbury class.

'My God, I wish they talked English in England,' he moaned. 'When I said pants, I meant what you aborigines call trousers.'

Mr Scarborough was openly amused. The misunderstanding brought a smile to his lips, quickly followed by apologies.

'I will return to G.H.Q. immediately and the error shall be rectified.'

'Would it be too much to ask you to fly like a bat out of hell? I've got a date.'

Mr Scarborough assured him that he would be back in twenty minutes, if not sooner, and his promise was fulfilled. This time there was no frustration or chagrin on Biff's part. He expressed his gratification wholeheartedly.

'Now you're talking,' he said. 'Now you've got the right idea. I'll take those and those. Oh, by the way, I shall have to ask you to chalk them up on the slate for the time being. I'm a little short of ready cash.'

Mr Scarborough took the blow very well. He showed nothing but gentle sympathy as he rewrapped his parcel. He gave Biff to understand that he mourned for him in spirit, but he was quite definite in his statement that head-quarters did not extend credit. Charm of manner, he made it clear, could never be accepted as a substitute for coin of the realm. Presently he was gone, taking his parcel with him, and the slough of despond closed over Biff once more. He sank into a chair and was still sitting there looking and feeling as if he had been sandbagged, when the telephone rang.

He went wearily to answer it, and a well-remembered voice spoke.

'Mr Christopher? Lord Tilbury speaking. I was wondering if you had thought over that matter we were discussing. What did you say?'

Biff had not spoken. The sound which had arrested Lord Tilbury's attention had been a gasp. Sudden, as the poet said, a thought had come like a full-blown rose, flushing his brow. It was several moments before he was able to speak.

'Yes,' he said, after his silence had caused his interlocutor to utter quite a number of testy 'Are you there's'. 'I've been giving the set-up a good deal of earnest meditation, and I'd very much like to have another talk with you. Could you pop over here?'

'Certainly. I will be with you immediately.'

'Well, young man,' said Lord Tilbury a few minutes later, 'I'm glad you seem to have come to your senses.'

Biff was not listening. He was scrutinizing his visitor,

estimating his girth and length of limb. The latter was satisfactory, the former, he felt, did not matter, for one can always take in a reef if necessary.

'Tilbury,' he said, 'I am a desperate man. Give me those pants of yours.'

CHAPTER NINE

THE discovery that Biff was safely back in Halsey Chambers and not in the custody of the police, indicating that all his subtle schemes had gone for nothing, had come as a shattering blow to Percy Pilbeam. It had caused the word to go around the Argus Agency that the boss was in ugly mood. The stenographer Lana had warned the stenographer Marlene to expect black looks and harsh words if summoned to the inner office to take dictation, and one of the firm's staff of skilled investigators, a Mr Jellaby, who had ventured into Percy's presence to make a report, had slunk out complaining of having had his head bitten off. It was what Spenser the office boy, a facile phrase-maker, described as a regular reign of terror.

And then Murphy had spoken of his friend Billingsley and his relations with the late Mr Pyke, and Percy had realized that all was not lost. It was with his equanimity completely restored that he had put in that second telephone call to Tilbury House. Recalling his own awe of Lord Tilbury in the old days, he was convinced that Biff would never be able to stand up against him if subjected to the full force of his dominant personality. All was well, he felt, and when Spenser the office boy entered to inform him that a gentleman was in the ante-room asking to see him, he greeted him cordially, much to the latter's relief, for he had been anticipating a fate similar to that of the recent Mr Jellaby.

'Gentleman named Christopher,' said Spenser, and Percy twirled his moustache in surprise. He could imagine no reason for this call. That Biff might have come to collect the forty pounds due to him for services rendered did not present itself as a possibility, for the promise to pay this sum had faded completely from Percy's mind. His memory was always inclined to be uncertain with regard to agreements not written, signed, witnessed and stamped at Somerset House.

When Biff was ushered in, he was amazed, as Jerry had been, by his air of well-being. Except for the sombre puffiness of his right eye and the fact that he was wearing trousers which did not begin to fit him, his visitor's aspect, considering that he had so recently been in session with Murphy, the human suction pump, was positively spruce. Nor was his voice the voice of one who has been wandering over the hot sands.

'Hi, Pilbeam o' man,' he said in a clear bell-like tone without a trace of roopiness in it. 'How's tricks?'

Percy replied that tricks were more or less as was to be desired, and said he noticed that Biff had sustained an injury to his eye.

'How did that happen?'

'Oh, just one of those things. Unavoidable on a night out.'

'I see. By the way, Lord Tilbury was asking for your phone number this morning. Did he ring you up?'

'He not only rang me up, he paid me a personal visit. He wanted to discuss the will of the late Edmund Biffen Pyke.'

'Ah! What had he to say about it?'

'He said he was going to contest it on the ground that the old boy was bonkers. Of course I laughed him to scorn. I told him he hadn't a hope.'

Percy shook his head, as a wise father might have done at a loved but too impulsive son.

'I'm not sure of that, if you don't mind me saying so. By the purest chance I happened to run into an American newspaper man who was acquainted with Mr Pyke. From what he told me, I thought it looked as if Tilbury might have a case. Did he mention Mr Pyke's habit of lunching backwards?'

'Sure. I thought it an excellent idea.'

'And Charles Fort?'

'That's right.'

'And he suggested making a settlement out of court?'

'Yes.'

'Well, I think you would be wise to do it. Better than letting yourself in for a law suit.'

'Gosh, I don't mind law suits. They open the pores and keep the arteries from hardening. He wouldn't have a dog's chance of winning. But why are you so interested?'

'Oh, no particular reason. I just don't like the idea of you losing all that money.'

'I won't. And while on the subject of money, Pilbeam o' man, I've come for mine.'

Percy winced. He remembered now that there had been some talk of money, and he braced himself to be strong.

'You said if I plied that international spy with drink, there would be forty pounds waiting for me at your office today. Well, today's today and here I am at your office. Out with the old cheque book, Pilbeam.'

Percy winced again, as he generally did when called upon to produce his cheque book.

'There was an agreement, I remember, yes. Did you manage to find out anything from that man?'

Biff was frank and manly about it. He descended to no subterfuges and evasions.

'Not a thing. I warned you I mightn't be able to. I did my best to draw him out. I worked the conversation around to Russia and said it must be most unpleasant there in the winter months when your nose turns blue and comes apart in your hands. He said Yes, he supposed it must be very disagreeable. I then asked him what Kruscheff was really like, and he said he had not met him. He said he had never been in Russia, the only time he had ever left England having been once on a day trip to Boulogne. These international spies are cagey. They play it close to their chests. He wasn't giving anything away. He talked about stamps most of the time.'

'Stamps?'

'He collects them. Just a front, of course.'

'How a front?'

'Use the loaf, Pilbeam. Naturally if a guy gives it out that he collects stamps, he lulls suspicion. You write him off as a harmless loony and don't bother any more about him. And all the time he's planning his plans and plotting his plots. Damn clever, these international spies.'

'So you found out nothing?'

'Only that he can mop the stuff up like a vacuum cleaner. His powers of suction are almost unbelievable. Even at Bleeck's in New York I've never seen anything to equal them, and Bleeck's, in case you don't know, is where the gentlemen of the American press go for their refreshment. I suppose in Russia they train these secret agents specially to acquire resistance to spirits and liquors. Steeped in vodka from early childhood, a fellow like this Murphy gets so that nothing alcoholic can shake his aplomb. I tell you, Pilbeam, long after I was seeing two of him, and that foggily, he was leaning back in his chair without even a flush on his face. I admired him intensely and would like to know him better. You raise your eyebrows? You disapprove? It shocks you that I should seek the friendship of a man like that? He is an enemy agent, you say, who at the drop of a hat would slip a stick of dynamite under the House of Commons and blow the members into the next parish. Well, why shouldn't he? Do them a world of good.'

Possibly because he was not in sympathy with this broad-minded attitude, or possibly for other reasons, Percy Pilbeam's manner took on a coldness which Henry Blake-Somerset would have admired.

'Then what it amounts to is that you accomplished nothing.'

'Not my fault.'

'I dare say. But in the circumstances you can hardly expect me to pay you forty pounds.'

'You were thinking of making it fifty?'

'I'm not going to pay you a penny.'

Biff tottered. His left eye, the one that had not been closed by enemy action, widened in a stare of horror and incredulity. The life he had led both in New York and Paris had left him aware that his fellow men were capable at times of work which could be classified as raw, but he had never supposed that it was possible for one of them to stoop to work as raw as this.

'You aren't?'

'No.'

'But I *need* it!'

'I can't help that.'

'So Jerry was right,' said Biff, shocked. 'He said you were a human rat and, considering everything, I call that flattering.'

'Spenser,' said Percy, who had pressed a bell, 'show this gentleman out.'

Biff did not pursue the argument. All his better feelings urged him to give Percy Pilbeam the shellacking his every action called for, but he realized that this must inevitably result in arrest for assault and battery. The bell, he knew, would scarcely have rung for the conclusion of the final round of the Christopher-Pilbeam bout before Percy would be sending out hurry calls for the police, and much as he now disliked Percy and would have enjoyed exterminating him, it was not a pleasure for which he was prepared to sacrifice several million dollars. Hotly as his sister Kay would have contested the statement, there were times when he could behave with prudence, and this was one of them. Seeming to shrink within himself, which was not a safe thing to do while wearing trousers as roomy as those of Lord Tilbury, he gave Percy a cold look and followed Spenser from the room, and Percy had started to give his attention once more to the matrimonial difficulties of Mrs F. G. Bostock, when the telephone rang.

'Pilbeam?'

'Tilbury?'

'Lord Tilbury speaking. I am at Number Three, Halsey Chambers.'

Odd, felt Percy. He would have expected him to have left there long ago.

'Bring me trousers, Pilbeam.'

'What?'

'Trousers, and be quick about it.'

'Why?'

'Never mind why,' said Lord Tilbury, his voice choking a little. 'Don't sit there asking questions. Bring me trousers.'

It was the poet Horace who, speaking in Latin as was the custom in the circles in which he moved, recommended the keeping of a calm mind in even the most trying circumstances. Aequam memento rebus in arduis servare mentem was the way he put it, and the general view has always been that his advice was sound. But he could not have sold this piece of philosophy to Lord Tilbury at this point in his career if he had argued with him a full hour by Shrewsbury clock. There was no ancient Roman stoicism about the first Baron as he awaited the coming of Percy Pilbeam.

The idea of appealing to Percy for help in the delicate situation in which he found himself had not been the first of those that had occurred to Lord Tilbury after Biff had left him. His initial impulse had been to telephone Gwendoline Gibbs at Tilbury House and request her to go to Barribault's Hotel and having made a selection from the trouserings in his room on the third floor to bring her choice to Halsey Chambers. What had caused him to reject this plan had been the thought of how the commission would diminish his stature in her eyes.

There is nothing, of course, actually low and degrading in losing one's trousers, especially if the loss is the result of force majeure and intimidation, but the man who does so unquestionably tends to become a figure of farce, and he shrank from the thought of appearing as a figure of farce to Gwendoline Gibbs. If there was one thing on which he was counting to win her love, it was his dignity, his importance. The revelation of what had occurred would no doubt give her a good laugh, but the last thing he desired was for her to have a good laugh at his expense.

He thought next of telephoning to his butler at Wimbledon, and was about to do so when he remembered that he had no butler at Wimbledon. That unfortunate outburst of peevishness which had caused his staff to turn in their portfolios had made a clean sweep of the domestic help. Like Mrs Bingley the cook, Clara the parlourmaid, Jane the housemaid and Erb the boy who cleaned the knives and boots and did odd jobs around the house, Willoughby the butler had left to seek employment elsewhere. He had vanished like the snows of yesteryear.

It was a galling situation for a man who owned twenty-three pairs of trousers to find himself in, and it is not too much to say that Lord Tilbury chafed. He had sometimes had nightmares in which the same sort of thing had happened to him, but he had never envisaged the possibility of being converted into a sans culotte in the daytime, and he was at a loss to know how to cope with the new experience. He was indeed on the point of abandoning hope, when there caught his eye the bright cover of a recent issue of *Society Spice* which its late editor had chanced one day to bring home with him, and he uttered a sound midway between a gurgle and a snort, a bronchial rendering of Archimedes's 'Eureka!'. He had been reminded of Percy Pilbeam.

His blood pressure, which had risen dangerously, fell. His mind, which had been a mere maelstrom of mixed emotions, ceased to gyrate. It amazed him that he had not thought of this solution of his difficulties earlier. He could not reveal his predicament to Gwendoline Gibbs, because he valued her opinion of him. He could not send out distress signals to Willoughby the butler, because for all practical purposes he had ceased to exist. But Pilbeam was still available, and for what Pilbeam might think on learning the facts he cared little. Possibly his former underling would be amused. If so, let him be amused. Lord Tilbury could imagine nothing of less consequence.

Thirty seconds later he was at the telephone and had begun the conversation which has just been recorded.

There followed a long period of waiting which caused his blood pressure to begin to rise again and his mind to become disordered once more. He was a man accustomed to having his commands not only obeyed but obeyed promptly. When he sketched out a course of action to a subordinate, he expected the latter to respond with something of the alacrity of a jet plane, and though Pilbeam was now independent, he still regarded him as a subordinate. He had told Pilbeam to be quick about it, and he was not being quick about it. This dallying irked him.

At long last the bell rang and he sprang to the door. It was Percy Pilbeam who stood without, and he was accompanied by a fine dog of the Boxer breed which endeavoured as far as its leash would allow to leap at him and cover his face with burning kisses, as is the habit of Boxers. Eluding its caresses, he spoke with stern reproach. He was annoyed, and he did not care if this underling of his knew it.

'What a time you have been, Pilbeam,' he said fretfully.

Percy seemed surprised and pained.

'I got here as soon as I could. I had to go all the way to Valley Fields to get Towser.'

'Towser?'

'You said you wanted him. The dog you gave Gwen.'

Lord Tilbury started violently.

'Are you by any chance alluding to Miss Gibbs?'

'Of course. Oh, I see what you mean. You're surprised that I call her Gwen. She's my cousin.'

It would be idle to pretend that this did not come as a shock to Lord Tilbury. It came as a substantial shock, all the more so because that very morning the waiter who had brought him his breakfast at Barribault's had confided in him how happy his niece Gwendoline was in her position as his, Lord Tilbury's, secretary. And it is proof of the depth of the latter's passion that these discoveries, though each had caused him to behave for an instant like a barefoot dancer who has inadvertently stepped on a tintack, did not weaken it to any noticeable extent. He would have been the first to admit that he would vastly have preferred not to become a cousin by marriage to Percy Pilbeam and not to have to go through life calling Mr Pilbeam senior Uncle Willie, but if those unpleasantnesses were involved in the package deal, he was prepared to put up with them. He merely registered a resolve that when he and Gwendoline were in their little nest, if you could call The Oaks, Wimbledon Common, that, both this private investigator and this third-floor waiter should be rigorously excluded from it. No open house for the Pilbeams, father and son, was the policy to which he proposed to cling.

'Oh?' he said, stepping back to foil another affectionate leap on the part of Towser, *né* Champion Silverboon of Burrowsdene. 'Is that so?', and added something about it being a small world. 'Pilbeam,' he said, returning to the main point from what was after all a side issue, 'you have made an idiotic blunder.'

'Oh?' said Percy, not without stiffness. He disliked being called idiotic.

'I want trousers – *trousers!*'

'I see you do,' said Percy. 'I noticed directly I came in that you hadn't any on, and I was wondering why.'

Lord Tilbury turned purple, his habit in moments of emotion.

'I will tell you why. That young scoundrel Christopher took mine from me. He threatened to assault me unless I gave them to him.'

'Why did he want them? Was he collecting trousers?'

'He had been deprived of his own. He explained that to me before he left. In order to prevent him going out and getting into trouble and forfeiting my brother's money, his sister took them away.'

'Ingenious,' said Percy Pilbeam, who was a man to give credit where credit was due. The thought crossed his mind that the Christophers were a family to be reckoned with. 'And what do you want me to do?'

Lord Tilbury clicked his tongue impatiently. He would have thought it was obvious what he wanted Percy to do.

'I want you to go to my house on Wimbledon Common and bring me another pair. You know my house on Wimbledon Common?'

'I can find it.'

'The trousers are in the wardrobe of my bedroom on the first floor,' said Lord Tilbury. He went to the table on which Biff had been considerate enough to empty the pockets of the purloined garments. 'Here is the front door key.'

Percy took the key and slipped it absently into his vest

pocket. His agile brain was busy with schemes for turning this situation to his financial benefit.

'I thought you had moved to Barribault's.'

'I have,' said Lord Tilbury, shuddering for a moment as he recalled that conversation on the hotel's third floor with the waiter who might ere long be his uncle by marriage. 'But most of my things are at Wimbledon. And if you think I am going to send you to Barribault's Hotel to ask at the desk if you may go up to my suite and get me a pair of trousers because I have been forcibly deprived of the ones I was wearing, you are very much mistaken. The story would be all over London in half an hour. So kindly stop talking like a fool, Pilbeam, and go to Wimbledon immediately.'

A purist might have considered his tone peremptory and his manner brusque. Percy Pilbeam was such a purist. He flushed beneath his pimples and his mouth set mutinously below its moustache, but he had not yet reached the stage of open defiance. Something of the awe with which his former employer had once affected him still lingered. It was only when Lord Tilbury went on to say 'Do you hear me, you idiot? What are you waiting for?' with an even more offensive intonation that he finally cast off the shackles. Who, he asked himself, was this old blighter to order him about? He spoke curtly.

'I haven't time to go to Wimbledon. I've a business to attend to.'

'Pilbeam!' said Lord Tilbury awfully, but Percy was now beyond intimidation. He had, moreover, thought of a way by which he could reap financial profit from the current situation. He had never to think for long when there was money in the offing.

'Oh, come off it, Tilbury,' he said. 'The trouble with you is that you've got so used to pushing people around that you think you can do it to everyone you meet, and then you run up against someone like me who doesn't give a tinker's curse for what you say or what you don't say and you get what's coming to you. I'll be blowed if I go slogging off to Wimbledon. I'll tell you what I will do, though, as you're an old friend. I'll sell you these trousers of mine. They'll be a tight fit, because you're what I'd call a stylish stout, but you'll be able to navigate in them as far as Barribault's. What do you say to that?'

A man who, starting from nothing, has built up a vast publishing enterprise is not long in learning the lesson that there are times when amour propre must be sacrificed to expediency. Not recently, but frequently in his early days, Lord Tilbury had been compelled to suppress his natural feelings and accept rebuffs. Printers and compositors had made what he considered monstrous demands, and he had yielded because there was no alternative. So now, though he turned purple and glared, he did not hesitate. His was a practical mind. He wanted trousers. Pilbeam had them, and that was all that mattered. He abated nothing of the desire he was feeling so strongly to skin the proprietor of the Argus Enquiry Agency with a blunt knife and dip him in boiling oil, but whatever he thought of him – and how Gwendoline Gibbs could possibly have a cousin like that was beyond his comprehension – he saw that his proposition must be accepted.

'How much?' he said.

'A hundred and ten pounds,' said Percy.

The shock was severe, and Lord Tilbury had every excuse for tottering. He seemed to see his former underling indistinctly through a heavy mist, which of course was the best way of seeing him. He reeled and might have fallen, had he not clutched at the Boxer Towser.

'You're insane!' he gasped.

'Not a bit of it,' said Percy equably. 'I'm doing you the trousers for ten quid and adding on the hundred I had to pay Christopher for going and drinking with Murphy.'

'I'm not going to pay that!'

'You certainly are.'

'A hundred pounds!'

'Necessary expense. It's a long story, but I had to make him think he was working for Scotland Yard and that was what they were giving him.'

'I won't pay it!'

'Just as you say. Come on, Towser.'

In the brief moment before he spoke again six alternative schemes for resolving this business disagreement darted through Lord Tilbury's mind. Each of them resembled the others in that they all had to do with somehow overpowering this mutinous ex-employee, stripping him of his trousers and going on his way triumphant. He was compelled to reject them all. Percy was no colossus, but then no more was he. The outcome of a physical struggle would be dubious. If he had had a stout club or a hatchet, something constructive might have been accomplished, but he had no club, no hatchet. As the editorial writers on his morning papers were always saying, it was necessary in these circumstances to bow with as good a grace as possible to the inevitable.

'Make it fifty, Pilbeam.'

'I'd be out of pocket.'

'Seventy-five.'

'No, but seeing you're an old friend I'll come down to the level hundred.'

Lord Tilbury argued no further. The healing thought had come to him that if he left Percy marooned in here, he could call at his bank and stop whatever cheque he might write. It was like a breath of cool air on his fevered brow.

'Very well,' he said, producing chequebook and fountain pen, and Percy was astounded by the cheerfulness of his tone. 'There you are,' he said, and a minute later, a ghastly sight from the waist downward, he was on his way to the door, to the regret of Champion Silverboon of Burrowsdene, who liked his looks and had hoped for a better acquaintance.

3

Lord Tilbury, like other men of substance, employed the services of several banks, dotted here and there about the metropolis. The one on which he had written the cheque he had given Percy was the Mayfair branch of the National Provincial only a short distance from Halsey Court, and it was thither that he now directed his steps – difficult steps, for the Pilbeam trousers were an unpleasantly snug fit, sticking closer than a brother. There had, indeed, been a moment when, lacking a shoe horn, he had almost despaired of getting into them.

From the bank, the cheque well and truly stopped, he proceeded to Barribault's Hotel, where he changed his clothes, and from Barribault's Hotel he telephoned his solicitor, commanding him to come immediately and lunch with him in the grill room. And in a few minutes, for his offices were in the next street, the solicitor presented himself.

London solicitors come in every size and shape, but they have this in common, that with a few negligible exceptions they all look like some species of bird. Jerry Shoesmith's Uncle John, for instance, that guiding spirit of Shoesmith, Shoesmith and Shoesmith of Lincoln's Inn Fields, resembled a cassowary, while elsewhere you would find owls, ducks, sparrows, parrots and an occasional ptarmigan. Lord Tilbury's legal adviser, a Mr Bunting of Bunting, Satterthwaite and Miles, could have mixed without exciting comment in any gathering of vultures in the Gobi Desert, though his associates would have been able to expose him as an impostor when meal time came, for unlike the generality of vultures he had a weak digestion and had to be careful what he ate. Lord Tilbury, himself a hearty trencherman, never enjoyed breaking bread with him owing to his habit of bringing medicine bottles to the table and giving a vivid description of what the dish he, Lord Tilbury, was consuming would do to his, Mr Bunting's, interior organs if he, Mr Bunting, were ever foolish enough to partake of it.

However, you cannot pick and choose when you are in need of a solicitor, you have to go to the man who knows his law, and Lord Tilbury had implicit faith in Mr Bunting's legal acumen. He would have preferred not to ask him to lunch, but time pressed, for owing to his sessions with Biff and Percy Pilbeam he had allowed a great deal of unfinished business to accumulate on his desk. So he issued the invitation, and in due course Mr Bunting appeared.

'Very fortunate you caught me in time, my dear Tilbury,' he said. 'I was just going out for my glass of milk when you telephoned. I always take a glass of milk at this hour, sipping it slowly. Am I right in supposing that there is some quillet of the law on which you wish to consult me?'

Lord Tilbury said there was, and led the way to their table. There, declining an offer to sniff at the contents of Mr Bunting's medicine bottle, the mere smell of which, Mr Bunting said, would give him some idea of what he had to put up with, he ordered a steak and fried potatoes, tut-tutted sympathetically when Mr Bunting told him what would happen if he himself ate a fried potato, and got down to what his guest would have called the *res*.

'An amusing point came up at Tilbury House this morning, Bunting. A short story was submitted to one of my editors in which a character, for reasons into which I need not go, was compelled by another character to give him his trousers.'

Mr Bunting sipped his milk slowly, and put a point.

'You use the word "compelled". Am I to understand that force was employed?'

'There were threats of force.'

'These trousers, then, were parted with under duress?'

'Exactly.'

'I see. Are you really going to drink beer with that steak, Tilbury?'

'Never mind my beer. Please listen.'

'Quite. I was only thinking what beer would do to me.'

'We like to get these things right in our magazines,' said Lord Tilbury, interrupting his guest as he spoke of acid ferment. 'Could he – the first man – have the other man arrested?'

'Summarily arrested?'

'Precisely. Go to a policeman and give him in charge.'

'The spinach here,' said Mr Bunting, who after finishing his milk and quaffing deeply from his medicine bottle had begun to pick at the vegetable mentioned, 'is exceptionally good. It is one of the few things I know I can digest. Asparagus, on the other hand, I regret to say, is sheer poison to me, while as for peas—'

Lord Tilbury shot him a look which, if it had been

directed at some erring minor editor of Tilbury House, would have reduced that unfortunate to a spot of grease.

'I should be obliged if you would listen to me, Bunting.'

'I beg your pardon. Certainly, certainly. You were saying?'

'I was asking you if depriving a man of his trousers is a felony for which an arrest can be made?'

Mr Bunting shook his head.

'It would be a matter for a civil action.'

'You're sure of that?'

'Quite sure. The case would be on all fours with that of Schwed versus Meredith, L.R. 3 H.L. 330, though there the casus belli was an overcoat. Schwed sued before the magistrates of South Hammersmith sitting in petty court and was awarded damages.'

Lord Tilbury choked on his steak. The disappointment had been severe. He had been so confident that his worries were over, his problems solved. He fell into a gloomy silence, from which he was jerked a moment later by a sudden ejaculation from his guest.

'See that fellow over there? See what he's eating? Hungarian goulash. Do you know what would be the effect on my bile ducts if I ate Hungarian goulash?'

For quite a while Mr Bunting spoke clearly and well on the subject of his bile ducts, but Lord Tilbury was not listening. His interest in his companion's interior was tepid, and in fairness to him it must be said that the revelations the solicitor was making were not of a kind to rivet the attention of any but a medical man. But he would in any case have been distrait, for a sudden idea had sprung into his mind and he was occupied in turning it over and examining it.

The quiet confidence with which Mr Henderson of Henderson, Henderson, Henderson, Henderson and Henderson had spoken at their recent meeting had had its effect on Lord Tilbury. He had maintained a bold front, but it was with the feeling that his position in the matter of contesting his brother's will was not a strong one that he had left Halsey Chambers, and when subsequently he had telephoned Biff suggesting another talk, it had merely been with the hope of swaying that young man with the strength of his personality. Legally he had felt insecure. He was wondering now if he had not been wrong in giving so much credence to Mr Henderson's pronouncements. It might well be that a man of that age had not yet acquired the firm grasp of the law of Great Britain possessed by an older and more experienced practitioner like this luncheon guest of his, who, whatever the shortcomings of his bile ducts, was recognized in legal circles as being at the top of his profession.

'Bunting,' he said.

'Eh?' said Mr Bunting, breaking off in the middle of a description of what he had once suffered in his hot youth when he, too, had eaten Hungarian goulash.

'You remember I consulted you in the matter of contesting my late brother's will.'

'Quite. I was of opinion that you had no evidence.'

'I think I have some now. If I invited you to lunch and insisted on our lunching backwards, what would you say?'

'Lunching backwards?'

'Exactly.'

'I don't understand you.'

'It's very simple. We would begin with coffee and cigars—'

'I never smoke cigars, only a type of health cigarette from which the nicotine has been extracted. They come, I believe, from Bulgaria and are aromatic and not only harmless but actively helpful in curing bronchial asthmas, duodenal ulcer, high blood pressure and—'

'Will you kindly *listen!*' boomed Lord Tilbury. 'I am speaking of this practice of my brother lunching backwards. I consider it strong proof of mental instability.'

'Your brother used to do that?'

'I can bring witnesses to testify to it,' said Lord Tilbury. Speaking in measured tones, he told the story of Billingsley of *Time* or possibly *Newsweek* and his mid-day meal at the house of the late Edmund Biffen Pyke. It took some time, for at the mention of almost every item on the menu Mr Bunting interrupted to give a word picture of what would occur inside him if he ate or drank *that*. But in due course the recital came to an end, and he put the vital question.

'What would you think if I suggested a lunch like that to you?'

'I should be extremely surprised.'

'Would you accept it as proof of insanity? If I died, would you, taking that lunch into consideration, feel that there were grounds for contesting my will?'

Mr Bunting, who had finished his spinach and was now drinking hot water, demurred.

'My dear Tilbury, I hardly think I would be prepared to go as far as that. I doubt if such an action would stand up in court. A good counsel would argue – and I think successfully – that these were merely a whimsical man's amiable eccentricities. Lunching backwards he would dismiss as an amusing pleasantry, and I think he would have the jury with him.'

'I'm sure there must have been cases where wills were contested on less evidence and won by the plaintiff.'

'On the motion picture screen, perhaps. Seldom, I imagine, in real life. What's the matter, Tilbury?'

He might well ask. There had proceeded from Lord Tilbury's lips a sort of gasping cry. It had been caused by those words "motion picture screen". They had acted on him like the stick of dynamite his employees had so often wished they could touch off under him. He had remembered Mr Llewellyn. So much had been happening to him of late that all thoughts of that sensitive Hollywood magnate had passed from his mind.

He sat for an instant congealed, then rose from his chair like a rocketing pheasant. Although he was a man built for endurance rather than speed, few athletes specializing in the shorter distances could have been out of the grillroom and at the telephone more quickly. Mr Bunting, gazing after him and remembering the dangerously unwholesome lunch he had made, supposed him to be in quest of a doctor and hoped he would not be too late.

It was with trembling fingers that Lord Tilbury dialled the number of Tilbury House.

'Miss Gibbs!'

'Yes, Lord Tilbury?'

'Did . . . did Mr Llewellyn call for me?'

'Oh yes, Lord Tilbury,' said Gwendoline brightly. 'He was very punctual.'

A sound like the bubbling cry of some strong swimmer in his agony escaped Lord Tilbury. He was picturing a deeply offended Llewellyn haughtily withdrawing pounds and pounds and pounds worth of advertising from the Tilbury papers.

'You did not think of . . . think up . . . happen to hit on an explanation of my absence?'

'Oh yes, Lord Tilbury. I told Mr Llewellyn you had suddenly been taken ill and were in bed at your house at Wimbledon.'

Relief did not make Lord Tilbury faint, but it came very near to doing so. He was conscious of a tidal wave of love and admiration for this pearl among girls, whose blonde beauty was equalled only by her ready resource. In every office at Tilbury House he had caused to be hung on the wall the legend 'Think On Your Feet,' and it looked to him as if Gwendoline Gibbs must have been studying them for months.

'Thank you, Miss Gibbs, thank you.'

'Not at all, Lord Tilbury.'

'So he went away quite happy?'

'Oh yes, Lord Tilbury. He was very sorry to hear you weren't well. He said he would be coming to Wimbledon as soon as he had had lunch to see how you were.'

'What!'

'That's what he said.'

'Oh, my God!'

'So don't you think you had better go there and be in bed when he arrives?'

Once more that tidal wave of love and admiration poured over Lord Tilbury. This girl, even though she might have an uncle who was a waiter and a cousin who shook one's belief in the theory that Man was Nature's last word, was fit to be the mate of the highest in the land, which he considered a reasonably good description of himself.

'Of course, of course. The only thing to do. Order the car and tell Watson to bring it to Barribault's without an instant's delay.'

'Very good, Lord Tilbury. Have you your key?'

'What key? Oh, the front door key? Yes, yes, of course I have it. No, by Jove, I haven't,' said Lord Tilbury, remembering the moment – how long ago it seemed – when he had given it to Percy Pilbeam. 'But there should be a spare one in the drawer of my desk. Would you go and look?'

'Certainly, Lord Tilbury. Yes,' said Gwendoline, returning, 'it was in the drawer. Shall I give it to Watson?'

'Do, Miss Gibbs, do. And thank you for being such a help.'

Lord Tilbury left the telephone booth thinking loving thoughts of Gwendoline Gibbs and hard ones of Ivor Llewellyn, whose persistence in seeking him out he considered tactless and officious. It was only as he was returning to his table in the grillroom that a shattering thought occurred to him. Who was going to admit Mr Llewellyn to his sick bed when the motion picture magnate arrived at the front door of The Oaks, Wimbledon Common?

For a moment the problem baffled him. He could not entrust this important assignment to Watson the chauffeur. Watson, like so many chauffeurs, suffered from slow mental processes and would be sure, when asked how his employer was, to reply that he had never been more solidly in the pink.

And then his eye fell on his legal adviser, who was still sipping the glass of hot water, so excellent for the digestive system, with which he always concluded a meal. An aromatic cigarette between his lips showed that he had armed himself well against bronchial asthmas, duodenal ulcers and high blood pressure.

'Bunting!' he cried, inspired.

'Ah, Tilbury. What did the doctor say?' asked Mr Bunting, all sympathy.

'I've got to go to bed.'

'I thought as much. That steak. That beer. Those fried potatoes. Give me your arm, and I'll help you to your room.'

'Not here. At my house at Wimbledon. I'll explain on the way there.'

'You want me to come with you?'

'Your presence is vital. I am supposed to be sick in bed there and I am expecting a very important advertiser to call in the course of the afternoon. I had a luncheon appointment with him today, and I forgot all about it. When he arrived at Tilbury House, my secretary with great presence of mind told him I had been suddenly taken ill and had had to be removed to Wimbledon, and he said he would be looking in there to see how I was. You understand my predicament?'

'Perfectly, my dear Tilbury. Are you sure this man will be calling at your house?'

'He told my secretary he would. He must find me in bed.'

'Quite. But why is my presence vital?'

'Somebody has to let him in. You must pose as the butler.'

Mr Bunting uttered a senile chuckle.

'I see what you mean. Of course I'll do it. You quite restore my youth, my dear Tilbury. As a young man I frequently appeared in amateur theatricals and, oddly enough, nearly always as a butler. Got some good notices, too. 'As Jorkins the butler Cyril Bunting was adequate' I remember the *Petersfield Sentinel* said on one occasion. Yes, you get to bed, Tilbury, and leave everything to me, confident that your affairs are in good hands.'

CHAPTER TEN

A PRIVATE investigator who takes his work with a proper seriousness, as Percy Pilbeam had always done, learns to accustom himself to long periods of waiting and inaction. In the early days of the Argus Agency, before a growing prosperity had enabled him to employ skilled assistants like Mr Jellaby and others, Percy had often stood for hours outside restaurants in the rain, waiting for some guilty couple to emerge and be followed to the love nest. The experience had given him several nasty colds in the head, but it had taught him patience, and it was in a composed frame of mind that he settled down to his vigil after Lord Tilbury had left him. Sooner or later, he presumed, somebody would be coming along to ease the strain of the situation, and until that happened there was nothing to be done but sit and relax. He took a chair and picked up the copy of *Society Spice* which had attracted Lord Tilbury's notice, shaking his head over the way the dear old paper had deteriorated since he had resigned the editorship. Dull, he felt. No zip, no ginger. In his time the word 'Spice' had meant something. Now it was a misnomer. If pieces like the one on Page Four about London's private gambling clubs were what modern readers considered spicy, he was sorry for them. The Boxer had fallen asleep, and the contents of *Society Spice* nearly made Percy follow his example.

What kept him from doing so was the uncomfortable feeling that there was a thought fluttering about the outskirts of his mind like a shortsighted dove seeking entry into a dovecot, and he could not pin it down.

It made him vaguely uneasy. He had the feeling that if this thought took shape and form, he would learn of something to his disadvantage. And then quite suddenly he got it. It was the recollection that in the way his former employer had perked up as he started to write that cheque there had been a suggestion of the sinister and disturbing. His manner had not been in character. Percy knew his Tilbury. However much the first Baron enjoyed writing the name that reminded him that he had acquired a title, he never enjoyed writing it at the bottom of a cheque for a hundred pounds. Yet on this occasion he had been cheerful, even chirpy. Instead of lingering over the task as if his every move distressed him, he had fairly dashed the thing off. His nib had flown over the paper.

There was, Percy was convinced, something fishy afoot, and abruptly he realized what it was. He had never made a study of extra-sensory perception, but he could tell what had been passing in Lord Tilbury's mind as clearly as if the latter had drawn a diagram for him. The old bounder was planning to stop that cheque, and here he, Percy, was, stuck in this flat and powerless to prevent him. His only hope was that the doublecrossing crook would have lunch before he went to the bank, feeling that with his payee confined to the premises of Number Three, Halsey Chambers, there was no need to hurry. That would give him time to reach the bank in advance of him, always assuming that he could secure trousers in which to make the journey.

But it was, he felt, a frail, sickly hope, and he uttered an expletive which disturbed the Boxer's slumber and caused him to raise an enquiring head. Obviously, in order to prevent Biff from leaving the flat, the female Christopher and her associate must have removed everything in the shape of trousers or their scheme would have been null and void. And it was not likely that either of them would return to the flat before they had had lunch. Percy slumped back in his chair, a broken man, and he was trying once more to interest himself in *Society Spice*, when an imperious hand pressed the front door bell. He caught up the Boxer's lead and went to the door. A slim, elegant young man was standing on the threshold.

'Good morning,' said this slim, elegant young man, speaking in a clipped, chilly voice which would have told Percy, if he had been better acquainted with the personnel of Embassies, that he was in the presence of a rising young diplomat with a future ahead of him in the diplomatic world. The thing about him that attracted Percy's attention was that he was wearing trousers, and his eyes gleamed covetously. He stared at those trousers. Travellers in India had gazed at the Taj Mahal with a less fascinated intensity.

There was nothing in Henry Blake-Somerset's manner, as he stood in the doorway, to indicate that he was seething with righteous indignation and resentment, for the first thing the authorities teach young diplomats is to look like stuffed frogs on all occasions in order to deceive foreigners. But he was so seething. He burned with a smouldering fury.

His mother, when he had told her of Kay's sudden departure for London, had been insistent that he take a firm line and have nothing more to do with a girl of whom she had disapproved at first sight and who could only be a hindrance to his career, but he was not at the moment prepared to go to quite this length. Love, or rather the tepid preference he felt for Kay, still animated the bosom beneath his well-cut waistcoat, and he proposed merely to give her a good talking to, showing her the error of her ways and strongly advising her to mend them. The scene he had in mind was to have been along the general lines of the interview between King Arthur and Guinevere at the monastery.

It was for the snake Shoesmith, the serpent who came breaking up homes before they even existed, that the lightning of his wrath was reserved. He intended to speak plainly to the man Shoesmith the moment the door opened. The spectacle, accordingly, of Percy Pilbeam, richly pimpled and wearing no trousers, had a disconcerting effect. His training would not allow him to gape, but he raised an eyebrow.

He was, however, soon himself again. You can startle a diplomat, but you cannot put him out of action.

'Is Mr Shoesmith in?' he asked, and his voice remained as controlled as ever. Nobody could have guessed how soiled it made him feel to be compelled to utter that name.

Percy Pilbeam did not reply. His gaze was still riveted on the trousers. He seemed to be in a sort of trance.

'This is the address from which he wrote to me,' said Henry, his voice becoming bleaker. He was feeling that Percy was just the sort of friend he would have expected

Shoesmith to have, but that did not mean that he had to put up with the impersonation he was giving of a deaf mute. 'He lives here, does he not?'

Percy came to himself with a start.

'Eh? Oh yes, he lives here, but he's out at the moment. Won't you come in? He ought to be back soon.'

Henry came in, eyeing Towser nervously as he did so. From childhood up he had always been uneasy in the presence of dogs, and he found the aspect of this one formidable beyond the ordinary. Boxers as a class rely for their appeal rather on their hearts of gold than on their looks, and Towser was no exception to this rule. Though inwardly all benevolence and camaraderie and good will, outwardly he was a canine Boris Karloff. One of his lower teeth had caught in his upper lip, and this, taken in conjunction with his protruding jaw and the dark circles under his eyes, gave him the appearance of a dog who would chew a man to the bone for tuppence. Indeed, he might even, Henry was feeling, preserve his amateur status by waiving the tuppence.

'Does he bite?' he asked apprehensively.

Percy seized on the question like an actor taking a cue. His agile mind had seen the way.

'Like a serpent,' he said. 'Always savage in captivity, these Boxers.'

'I hope you have a tight hold on him.'

'For the moment, yes,' said Percy, 'and it's just possible that I may be able to control him. It all depends on whether you give me your trousers.'

At this, Henry raised both eyebrows. It was a thing he did not often do, one generally being enough, but these words had struck him as so bizarre that he felt justified in giving the speaker the full treatment.

'I beg your pardon?'

'I want those trousers. I've got to get out of here and get out quick. There's a man on his way to the bank to stop a cheque he's given me, and if I don't get there ahead of him, I'll lose a hundred pounds. Put it this way. I need trousers and you don't, at least for the moment. You came here to see Shoesmith, and you can see him just as well without your trousers on. I'll stop in at a shop after I've been to the bank and buy you another pair and send them round. Think on your feet,' said Percy, remembering the slogan which had hung on his office wall in the days when he had been the editor of *Society Spice*.

Henry thought on his feet. He had seldom thought more rapidly. But though he accepted the situation, he made no pretence of liking it.

'I will give you these trousers—'

'That's the way to talk.'

'—but under protest.'

'That's all right. Give me them under anything you like,' said Percy Pilbeam spaciously, and a few minutes later was gone on winged feet, the dog Towser gambolling beside him. They made a cheery pair.

But though the dumb chum's cheeriness continued undiminished, that of Percy expired with a gurgle shortly after he had entered the premises of the Mayfair branch of the National Provincial Bank. His jaw and spirits sank simultaneously when the official behind the counter informed him that the cheque which he was presenting had been stopped on instructions from drawer. He also requested him politely but firmly to remove that dog.

Percy removed the dog. He took Towser to the office of the Argus Agency, deposited him there in the care of Lana and Marlene, the stenographers, curtly ordered Spenser the office boy to go out and buy a pair of trousers and take them to the gentleman at Three Halsey Chambers, and then, seating himself at his desk, dialled the number of Tilbury House.

His cousin Gwendoline answered the telephone.

'Gwen? Percy.'

'Oh, hullo, Perce.'

'Put me through to Tilbury.'

'He isn't here.'

'Where is he?'

'He's gone to Wimbledon. Shall I tell him you were asking for him?'

'No,' said Percy, and his voice was full of menace. 'I'll see him at Wimbledon.'

2

Custom, despite the opinion of the orator Burke, who said it did, does not always reconcile us to everything. Henry Blake-Somerset, to take an instance ready to hand, ought by now to have become reconciled to the sort of bereavement which had just befallen him, for it was the third of its kind that had disturbed the correct tenor of his life. Twice during his career as an undergraduate at Oxford University he had been boisterously de-trousered by rowing hearties in their cups, for his was a personality which for some reason grated on rowing hearties, especially when the vine leaves were in their hair, and one might have expected him to look on what had happened as pure routine.

Nevertheless, there was no suggestion of quiet acceptance of the position in his manner as he heard the door close behind Percy Pilbeam. He derived little comfort from Percy's parting promise to send in replacements, for there was that about the head of the Argus Enquiry Agency that generally failed to inspire confidence in those to whom he promised things. In speaking those words of cheer, he felt, Percy had merely been making conversation, and it was in black mood that he now began to pace the floor, what there was of it, walking with a fevered restlessness. Except that such an animal would not have been wearing what to Mr Scarborough of Cohen Bros – though not to Biff – were pants, there was a distinct resemblance between him and a caged tiger.

He had been moving to and fro for some time, still in a frame of mind of which a philosopher would have disapproved, when he chanced to look out of the window, and what he saw made him catch his breath in sharply. A taxi cab had drawn up at the entrance to Halsey Chambers and from it were alighting the man Shoesmith and Kay.

The sight appalled him. It was only too plain that in another minute or so he would have them with him, and though he had come to London with the express purpose of speaking his mind to both of them, he shrank from doing it in knee-length underlinen. The one thing the mind-speaker needs, if he hopes to impress himself on his audience, is to be decently clad from the waist downward. One or two of the old Greek and Roman orators may have got by in tunics, but it cannot have been easy.

The British diplomatic service trains its personnel well. It teaches them to think quickly in an emergency. Where another man in his place would have stood baffled, Henry acted. There was a door to his right, presumably that of a bedroom, and he was through it before one could have said 'Agonizing reappraisal'. It swung open an inch or two, but he did not risk closing it, for already key had sounded in lock and there were footsteps in the room he had left.

There was also silence, and this surprised him somewhat, for his experience of these two had been that when they got together they were always full of conversation – in his opinion far too full. He had no means of knowing that all through lunch at Previtali's, Oxford Street, the home-wrecker Shoesmith had been pleading with Kay to marry him and that she had told him she was giving the matter thought. A girl who is thinking does not prattle.

It was the homewrecker who was the first to speak.

'Biff seems to be in his room.'

'The best place for him.'

'Getting a little sleep.'

'He's certainly earned it.'

'Shall I have a look?'

'No, you might wake him.'

Silence again, broken at length by the wrecker of homes.

'Well?'

'Yes?'

'Have you made up your mind?'

'I'm still thinking. Let's hear from you again.'

'Very well, I love you, dammit.'

'Satisfactory so far. Carry on from there.'

It is always unpleasant for a man to have to listen to a comparative stranger proposing marriage to his fiancée, and even aesthetically Henry did not enjoy the performance. When he had proposed to Kay, it had been in a restrained, dignified manner in keeping with the traditions of the British Foreign Office, and this Shoesmith was being loud and incoherent and raucous. A torrent of words proceeded from him, and worse was to follow, for suddenly he ceased to speak and there came to Henry's ears a curious shuffling sound as if a wrestling bout were in progress, causing him first to start, then to quiver in every limb. He tried not to believe his ears, but unsuccessfully. If this man Shoesmith was not embracing Kay, kissing Kay, behaving to Kay in a quite unsuitable manner, he told himself, he, Henry, would be very much surprised.

His diagnosis was correct. When Kay spoke again, it was with the breathlessness of a girl who has been subjected to the type of wooing recommended by that recognized expert, her brother Edmund Biffen.

'Wow!' she said.

It was, in Henry's opinion, the wrong thing to say, and he did not like the tone in which she said it. There was, to his mind, a most uncalled-for suggestion of happiness in the ejaculation. It was the 'Wow!' of a girl whose dreams have come true and who has found the pot of gold at the end of the rainbow. Incredible though it might seem, it was plain to him that Kay, so far from being shocked, horrified and outraged, had been a willing participant in what, from where he stood, had sounded like a Babylonian orgy of the worst type, the sort of thing that got King Belshazzar talked about.

'You can let me go now,' she said. 'You've made your point.'

The conversational exchanges that followed would undoubtedly have nauseated Henry, had he been following them. But he was not giving them his attention. His thoughts were elsewhere. He was remembering what his mother had said. She had warned him against this girl, telling him that it was not too late to extricate himself from a most undesirable entanglement. And though he had protested that she was quite mistaken in her estimate and that a natural nervousness had prevented her from seeing Kay at her best, she had left him half persuaded. He saw now how right her woman's intuition had been, and he was conscious of a sensation not far from relief. He felt he had had an escape. He was a man who liked an orderly existence, and Kay, whatever her superficial charms, was manifestly a girl who preferred her existences disorderly. He may also have had the thought that now he would not have to have Edmund Biffen Christopher as a brother-in-law.

In the other room conversation was still proceeding. The man Shoesmith, after a series of incoherent observations, had become momentarily silent, as if exhausted by his emotions, and it was Kay who spoke.

'I suppose you know we're both crazy.'

'I don't follow you.'

'Rushing into it like this. You don't know a thing about me, and I don't know a thing about you.'

'My life's an open book. Left an orphan at an early age. Sent by my Uncle John in his capacity of guardian to Marlborough and Cambridge. Came down from Cambridge and messed about in Fleet Street for awhile. Got that New York correspondent job. Was fired. Became a Tilbury House wage slave and was fired again. Of course, I know what's in your mind. It will have struck you that every time we meet I've just lost my job, and this will have led you to feel that I'm a dubious proposition breadwinnerwise. But conditions will be very different from now on. Biff's going to buy the *Thursday Review* and put me in as editor, and that's a job I can hardly fail to hold down. I'm not likely to fire myself. If at first I make a mistake or two, I shall be very lenient and understanding.'

Kay was looking thoughtful.

'I wish our future didn't depend so on Biff. It makes me uneasy.'

Jerry begged her to correct this pessimistic streak of hers. The future, in his opinion, was rosy.

'Biff can't get into trouble now. There are only a few more days to go.'

'He can do a lot in a few days.'

'Not if he doesn't stir from the flat, and he can't stir from the flat.'

'Yes, that's true.'

'Don't have a moment's concern about Biff. And talking of Biff, I think we ought to let him know about us.'

'But he's asleep.'

'He won't be long.'

It had been Jerry's intention, when he flung open the door of his future relative's bedroom, to rouse him from his slumbers with a cheery shout, but this shout was never uttered. What actually emerged from his lips was a gurgling sound like that made by bath water going down a waste pipe.

'He's gone!'

'He can't have gone!'

'Well, look for yourself.'

'But how can he have gone?'

It was a question Jerry found himself unable to answer. He had read of Indian fakirs who had acquired the knack of disembodying themselves and reassembling the parts at some distant spot, but he could not bring himself to credit Biff with this very specialized ability. The only solution seemed to be that he had gone out in the demi-toilette in which Jerry had left him, and the thought froze the latter's blood. It was consequently a relief when Kay put forward another theory.

'You must have overlooked a spare pair he'd hidden somewhere.'

'Of course. You're perfectly right. I thought I saw a crafty look in his eye as I went out, as if he had an ace up his sleeve.'

'But where can he have gone?'

Illumination came to Jerry.

'I know! He was telling me that he had to get out of here so that he could go and see Linda Rome and heal what he called the breach.'

'Had he quarrelled with Linda?'

'She had quarrelled with him. Apparently she saw him having a tête-à-tête with Tilbury's secretary.'

'A blonde?'

'Very much so.'

Kay sighed.

'He's suffered from blonditis all his life. But I did hope he was cured.'

'He is. This was just a farewell meeting, designed not to hurt the girl's feelings. He was anxious to go and explain that to Linda Rome.'

'I wish you had let him. He couldn't get into any trouble if he was with Linda. She's a sobering influence. I've known Biff to become only half-crazy when under her spell.'

'She sounds a nice girl.'

'She's very nice, and she's got Biff hypnotized. If she tells him not to make a chump of himself, he doesn't make a chump of himself, though you'd hardly believe such a thing possible. I'll go and ask her if she's seen him. The place where she works is only a block or two away.'

'Be careful crossing the street.'

'I will.'

'Don't go talking to strange men or letting strange women give you candy.'

'I won't.'

'Watch out for simooms, earthquakes and other Acts of God, and hurry back as quick as you can, because every second you're not with me is like an hour. I love you, I love you, I love you, I love you,' said Jerry, putting it in a nutshell. 'Have you ever been struck by a thunderbolt?'

'Not that I remember. Have you?'

'Oddly enough, no. But every time you look at me with those eyes of yours, I feel as if I'd caught one squarely in the solar plexus. They're like twin stars.'

'Well, that's fine.'

'I like it,' said Jerry.

Nauseating, felt Henry Blake-Somerset, nauseating. He stared bleakly at the wall paper and began to rub his legs. His wrath remained hot, but his legs were cool and beginning to get chilly.

It seemed to Jerry, as he sat awaiting Kay's return, that a most unusual number of violets and daffodils were sprouting through the carpet and that the air had become unexpectedly full of soft music, played, if his ears did not deceive him, by those harps and sackbuts of which Biff had spoken in his conversation with the elder Pilbeam. He had been happy before in his life, but he had never touched such heights of ecstasy as now. This, he supposed, was more or less what Heaven would be like, though even Heaven would have to extend itself in order to compete.

The only thing that marred his feeling of well-being was Kay's absence. She had been gone now, he estimated, about six hours and he yearned to see her again. When the bell rang, he leaped to the front door with a lissom bound, only to have the words of welcome wiped from his lips by the sight of a small boy in a bowler hat, and not a particularly attractive small boy, at that. Spenser of the Argus Enquiry Agency, though of polished manners, was no oil painting. He had a snub nose, and he was heavily spectacled. Jerry, encountering his goggle-eyed gaze, had the illusion that he was being inspected through the glass of an aquarium by some rare fish.

'Good afternoon,' said Spenser. 'Are you the gentleman?'

This perplexed Jerry.

'Eh?' he said. 'What gentleman?'

'The gentleman I've brought the trousers for.' Blushing a little at having ended a sentence with a preposition, Spenser corrected himself. 'The gentleman for whom I have brought the trousers.'

'My name's Shoesmith.'

'Mine is Spenser. Lionel Spenser. Pleased to meet you, Mr Shoesmith.'

'I mean, are they for me?'

'That I could not say, sir. I was merely instructed by Mr Pilbeam to buy trousers and bring them to this address.'

'Mr Pilbeam?'

'Yes, sir. I am in his employment.'

'And he told you to bring me trousers?'

'He did not specify the recipient. Buy trousers and take them to Three, Halsey Chambers were his exact words.'

Jerry clutched his forehead. If asked, he would have admitted frankly that the intellectual pressure of the conversation had become too much for him.

'You're sure there's no mistake?'

'Quite sure, sir. Mr Pilbeam's instructions were most explicit.'

'All right. Put them on the table.'

'Very good, sir.'

'And here,' said Jerry, producing a half crown.

'Coo!' said Lionel Spenser, suddenly becoming human. 'Thanks a million.'

'No, on second thoughts,' said Jerry, 'better take them back to the shop and get your money refunded.'

Nestling in his bedroom retreat, Henry Blake-Somerset had listened to these exchanges with a growing impatience, eager to lay his hands on the manna in the wilderness which had descended so unexpectedly from the skies and resentful of all this chit-chat in the doorway which was postponing his hour of release. He had not intended to make his presence known until Lionel Spenser had gone on his way, for he knew that small boys, seeing a man in knee-length meshknit underwear, were apt to mock and scoff, but when he heard Jerry make this appalling suggestion, he realized that there was no time for delay. Even at the expense of amusing Lionel, he must issue a statement.

'Those trousers are for me,' he said.

There are few things that offer a greater test to the nervous system than a disembodied voice speaking in one's immediate vicinity, and both Jerry and Lionel Spenser leaped several inches from the ground, each suffering a passing illusion that the top of his head had broken loose from its moorings. There was bewilderment in Jerry's eyes as they met Lionel's and an equal bewilderment in Lionel's as they met Jerry's. Had those men in the employment of stout Cortez, whom the poet Keats has described as looking at each other with a wild surmise, been watching them, they could have picked up some useful hints in the way of technique.

'Did you hear something?' said Jerry in a whisper.

'Somebody spoke,' said Lionel, his voice hushed.

'I spoke,' said Henry Blake-Somerset, emerging from the bedroom with a cold dignity which almost compensated for the peculiarity of his appearance. He took up the parcel, gave Jerry a long, lingering look, and withdrew.

'Crumbs!' said Lionel Spenser, and Jerry agreed that 'Crumbs!' was the mot juste.

By the time Henry returned, fully clad and looking, as the song has it, like a specimen of the dressy men you meet up west, Jerry had managed to rid himself of his initial impression that what he had seen had been the Blake-Somerset astral body, but this had not brought ease of mind. What was exercising him now was the problem of finding the right thing to say. It is always difficult to strike just the correct conversational note when meeting a man to whose fiancée you have recently become betrothed. A certain *gêne* is inevitable.

Fortunately Henry appeared not to be in the vein for small talk. In silence he passed through the room, in silence opened the front door. There, turning, he gave Jerry another look which would have lowered the temperature even on the Yukon, and was gone.

It was perhaps five minutes later that the front door bell rang again.

The visitor this time was a pleasant-faced, capable looking girl in her late twenties. Jerry liked her at sight.

'Good afternoon,' she said. 'Are you Mr Shoesmith?'

After the emotional upheaval caused by his dealing with Lionel Spenser and Henry Blake-Somerset, Jerry might have been excused for not feeling quite sure, but after a moment's thought he was able to reply that he was.

'I hope I'm not interrupting you when you're busy, but I wanted to see you about Biff.'

Enlightenment came to Jerry.

'Are you Mrs Rome?'

'Not at the moment. I used to be, but the name now is Mrs Christopher.'

'What!'

'Biff and I were married this morning at the registrar's. I hope a marriage is legal when the bridegroom has a black eye. The registrar apparently thought it was all right, though from the way he kept looking at Biff and then shooting a glance at me I could see he was feeling we were beginning our married life in the wrong spirit.' She regarded Jerry with gentle concern. 'You seem stunned.'

Jerry admitted that she had surprised him a little.

'I was only thinking it was a bit sudden.'

'Why sudden? Biff and I have been engaged for a long time – on and off.'

'Of course, yes. But when you were speaking to me on the phone yesterday, I should have said off was the operative word.'

She laughed. A pleasant laugh, Jerry considered. Not in Kay's class, of course, but, as Mr Bunting would have said, adequate.

'Oh, was it you I talked to? Yes, I can understand you jumping to conclusions. But ... how long have you known Biff?'

'For years. He's about my best friend.'

'Then you must know he's the sort of cheerful idiot child nobody could be furious with for long. He came round to the place where I work this morning, and of course in a couple of minutes I'd forgiven him everything, and when he said "Let's get married right away", I said "Terrific", so off we went to the registrar's. Biff has a way with him.'

'He certainly has. Well, I'm delighted.'

'So am I, though I shall be happier when we're safe aboard that boat. We're off to America tomorrow.'

'You are?'

'Yes, I thought it was the prudent move.'

'I see what you mean. Even Biff can't get himself arrested in mid-ocean. Unless, of course, he goes in for barratry or mutiny on the high seas.'

'I'll be very careful to see that he doesn't.'

'I'm sure you will. Kay was saying only just now what a good influence you were on him.'

'Oh, is Kay in London?'

'She arrived last night to help me keep an eye on Biff. She went to see you. Didn't she find you?'

'No, I was at Wimbledon. I took Biff to my uncle's house. He was rather nervous because he thought the police might be after him and he wanted a hideaway. I thought The Oaks would be as good as any. There's nobody there. I was planning to join him tonight, and tomorrow morning we would have driven to Southampton. But a difficulty has arisen.'

'What's that?'

'I happened to want to ask my uncle something just now, and I rang up Tilbury House, and his secretary told me he was on the point of leaving for Wimbledon.'

'Oh, my gosh!'

'Yes, it would be an awkward meeting, wouldn't it? So will you take my car and drive down there and bring him back here? I've got the car outside. I can't go myself, because I shall be busy all the afternoon shopping. Biff needs a complete trousseau. He's very short of clothes.'

'I have some trousers of his at my uncle's place at Putney. You see, Kay and I thought he would be better without them.'

'You have nudist views?'

'We wanted to keep him tied to the flat so that he couldn't go out and get into trouble.'

'I see. Well, I don't think we need bother about those. I'll get him everything he needs.'

'And you're really sailing tomorrow?'

'We are, if the hand of the law doesn't fall on Biff before then. I've got the tickets, and fortunately I have my visa. Mr Gish was thinking of sending me to New York, so I got it and everything's fine. By the way, did Biff tell you what it was he did last night?'

'Not a word, except that he got into a fight.'

'I gathered that the moment I saw him. Well, I must rush,' said Linda, and was gone, leaving Jerry profoundly relieved. Mrs Edmund Biffen Christopher had made a deep impression on him. She was a girl who inspired confidence.

He was about to go out to the car, when the bell rang.

'Good afternoon, sir,' said the policeman who stood on the mat. 'Sorry to trouble you, but could you tell me if a gentleman who looks like a dachshund lives here?'

CHAPTER ELEVEN

STANDING in the hall of The Oaks, Wimbledon Common, and taking in his surroundings with an appraising eye, Biff had become conscious of a cloud darkening his normally cheerful outlook on life. All the houses on Wimbledon Common are large, having been built in the days when householders did not consider home was home unless they had families of ten and domestic staffs of fourteen, and Lord Tilbury's little nest was in keeping with those of his neighbours. Outwardly it was of a nature to cause sensitive architects, catching sight of it, to stagger back with a hand over their eyes, uttering faint moans, while inside it was dark and gloomy and had depressed Biff from the moment his wife had left him.

Alone in this vast, echoing mansion, he had begun to feel like Robinson Crusoe on his island. He had, as he had told Jerry, dined here once or twice, but on those occasions there had been, in addition to other guests, butlers and maids and similar fauna bobbing about. It was the solitude that weighed on his nervous system. He felt apprehensive and in the grip of a despondency of the kind that can be corrected only with the help of a couple of quick ones, and it was not long before the thought floated into his mind that Lord Tilbury, his unconscious host, possessed a cellar and that the key to that cellar would presumably be hanging on its hook in the butler's pantry.

He found the key. He opened the cellar door. And there before him were bottles and bottles nestling in their bins, each one more than capable of restoring his mental outlook to its customary form. And he was in the very act of reaching out for the one nearest to hand, when Linda's face seemed to rise before his eyes and he remembered his promise to her. 'Lay off the lotion,' she had said to him, or words of that general import, and he had replied that he would. Even if the Archbishop of Canterbury were to come and beg him to join him in a few for the tonsils, he had said, no business would result.

He could not betray her trust. He had pledged his word. Furthermore, it was only too probable that when she joined him that night she would sniff at his breath. With a sigh he turned away and to divert his mind started to explore the house. He found himself in what he remembered to be the drawing-room, but greatly changed since his last visit, for its chairs and sofas were now swathed in dust sheets. The spectacle it presented was not exhilarating, and he did not spend much time looking at it. Scarcely had he passed through the door when the fatigue due to insufficient sleep on the previous night swept over him. He was just able to reach the nearest sofa before his eyes closed, and after that a salvo of artillery would probably not have woken him.

The arrival of Percy Pilbeam in a taxi cab did not even cause him to stir. Though this was perhaps not remarkable, for Percy, letting himself in with the key Lord Tilbury had given him, made very little noise. From long habit private investigators learn to be quiet in their movements, for when you are shadowing erring husbands to love nests, the less you advertise your presence, the better. Cats prowling at dusk could always have learned much from Percy, and family spectres would have benefited by taking his correspondence course. He closed the front door without a sound and, as Biff had done, stood looking about him. And as he looked, the militant spirit in which he had embarked on this expedition began to ebb.

Percy, unlike Biff, had never been inside The Oaks, Wimbledon Common, and its gloomy magnificence had an even more lowering effect on him than it had had on his fellow visitor. He had come here full of fire and fury, grimly resolved to extract another cheque from Lord Tilbury if he had to choke it out of him with his bare hands, but now he was beginning to wonder if he were equal to the task. In his office at the Argus Agency and in the homely surroundings of Number Three Halsey Chambers he had had no difficulty in being airy with Lord Tilbury, in defying Lord Tilbury and making it clear to him that a Pilbeam was a man to be reckoned with and not to be put upon, but the conviction was stealing over him that on the other's home grounds such an attitude would be harder to take. To use an expression which Lionel Spenser would never have permitted himself, Percy was beginning to get cold feet.

In these circumstances it was perhaps only natural that his thoughts should have taken the same direction as those of Biff. A voice had whispered to Biff that aid and comfort lay behind that cellar door, and the same voice, or one very like it, whispered the same thing to Percy Pilbeam.

The suggestion was well received. Pausing merely to give his moustache a twirl, he hastened cellarwards and was rejoiced to find that some careless hand had left the key in the lock. It was as he went in and stood gazing on the bottles that confronted him, trying to decide which one should have his patronage, that Lord Tilbury's Rolls Royce, chauffeur Watson at the wheel, purred in at the drive gates.

2

Mr Bunting was the first to alight, and having done so he winced as if he had seen some dreadful sight, as indeed he had.

'Good gracious,' he said. 'What a perfectly ghastly house. It looks like a municipal swimming bath.'

'Well, I didn't build it,' said Lord Tilbury shortly. He resented criticism of his belongings. 'Take the car back, Watson.'

'Isn't the chauffeur going to wait?'

'Of course he isn't going to wait. I'm supposed to be sick in bed, not gallivanting about in cars. I'll go to bed at once. There's no knowing when that damned Llewellyn will get here. Can I rely on you to play your part, Bunting?'

Mr Bunting drew himself up with the haughtiness one would have expected in a depictor of butlers whose ability in that direction, so highly praised by the *Petersfield Sentinel*, has been questioned. He replied coldly that Lord Tilbury need have no anxiety on the point, and Lord Tilbury went up to his bedroom.

His mood, as he undressed and put on a suit of yellow pyjamas with purple stripes, was ruffled and rebellious. A proud man, he resented having to behave like a hunted stag in order to keep on good terms with a mere Hollywood magnate, and the slow passing of time after he was between the sheets did nothing to improve his outlook. Impossible, he felt, even to smoke, and it was with a sigh of relief that after an eternity he heard footsteps approaching. The door opened, and he closed his eyes.

'Ah, Llewellyn,' he said in a weak voice. 'How good of you to come and see me.'

'Wrong number,' said Mr Bunting. 'This is Jorkins, the butler.'

The tedium of waiting had made Lord Tilbury somewhat petulant.

'What did you disturb me for? I was trying to get to sleep.'

'After that heavy lunch? Very injudicious. That's how you get liver trouble. It leads to splenic anaemia, where the spleen is enlarged and later the liver, from cirrhotic changes. An accumulation of fluid in the abdominal cavity—'

'Go away,' said Lord Tilbury.

'You don't want to hear about splenic anaemia?'

'No.'

'Just as you please. It's an absorbing subject, but if you would prefer not to be informed about it, that is entirely your affair. What I do think will interest you is the discovery I have made that the house is congested with burglars.'

He was right. It interested Lord Tilbury extremely. He sat up like a jack-in-the-box.

'What!'

'I am sorry,' said Mr Bunting. 'I was guilty of an inexactitude. "Congested" was perhaps too strong a word, suggesting as it does serried ranks of burglars. I've only found a couple so far. No doubt there are others in every nook and cranny, but the only ones I've managed to locate at present are the fellow in the cellar—'

Lord Tilbury uttered a strangled cry. His cellar was very

dear to him and he resented intruders on those sacred precincts.

'There is a burglar in the cellar?'

'He was in the cellar. I locked him in.'

'Telephone for the police!'

'I did. They came and took him away just before I looked in on you.'

'Excellent, Bunting. Well done.'

'I think I was adequate,' said Mr Bunting modestly. 'It would have been neater and more dramatically right to have had the police take both men away, but I did not find the other one till I was having a ramble through the house after they had left. He was asleep in the drawing-room.'

'Of all the impudence! Did you overpower him?'

'My dear Tilbury, when you get to my age, you don't overpower burglars. I let him sleep on. I hadn't the heart to disturb him.'

'I'll disturb him,' said Lord Tilbury, leaping from his bed in a flash of yellow and purple, and Mr Bunting agreed that it was perhaps time that the reveillé was sounded. He suggested that Lord Tilbury should arm himself with something solid from the bag of golf clubs which was standing in a corner of the room. He recommended the niblick, and Lord Tilbury felt that it was a wise choice. He had had no previous experience of intimidating a burglar, but instinct told him that it was a niblick shot.

And so it came about that Biff, roused from slumber by a hand that gripped his arm and shook it, opened his eyes drowsily. Seeing a stout man in yellow and purple pyjamas, accompanied by a dim something that looked like a vulture, and naturally supposing that this was merely a continuation of the nightmare he had been having, he closed them again and turned over on his side. It was only when his host's niblick descended smartly on an exposed portion of his person that the mists of sleep shredded away and he sat up, blinking.

'Oh, hello,' he said. 'So there you are.'

Lord Tilbury was too overcome to speak. What held him for the moment dumb was not righteous indignation at the discovery that a young man whom he particularly disliked had invaded his home and gone to sleep in his drawing-room without so much as a by-your-leave or with-your-leave. What was interfering with his vocal cords was the surge of emotion that comes to punters on race courses who see the long shot on which they have invested their shirts roll in lengths ahead of the field. His enemy had been delivered into his hands. No question of civil actions here. If ever there was a case for summary arrest, this case was that case.

Speech returned to him. He wheeled round on Mr Bunting.

'Bunting, can I have this man arrested for breaking and entering?'

'Unquestionably, if he did break and enter.'

'Well, I didn't,' said Biff. 'My wife let me in with her key.'

'You are a married man?' said Mr Bunting, interested.

'I was married this morning.'

'And may I ask how your wife came to be in possession of a key to my house?' enquired Lord Tilbury.

'She lives here. She's your niece Linda.'

'What!' cried Lord Tilbury, reeling.

'Hell's bells,' said Biff, 'if a wife can't offer her husband the hospitality of the house where she lives, things have come to a pretty pass. And what the devil are you doing in pyjamas at this time of day?'

Lord Tilbury did not reply. The sunshine had been blotted from his life. It was not only the thought of his niece's disastrous marriage that held him silent. He was musing bitterly on Providence. A moment before, he had been telling himself that Providence, always on the side of the good man, had gone out of its way to ensure that he should prosper as he deserved, and Providence, he now saw, was not the Santa Claus he had supposed but a heartless practical joker who raised the good man's hopes only to dash them to the ground. A moment before, it had seemed that a mere telephone call to the local police station was all that was needed to rule Edmund Biffen Christopher out of the race for the Pyke millions and life had been roses, roses all the way. Now it was dust and ashes. Not for an instant was he able to doubt the truth of Biff's story. What had induced Linda to marry him remained a mystery, and why she should have brought him here he could not say, but she had unquestionably done both of these things, and he shook with baffled fury like the villain in an old-time melodrama.

'Get out!' he shouted.

Biff raised his eyebrows.

'Did I hear you say Get out?'

'You did. This house is mine, not Linda's, and I don't want you in it.'

'Okay, if that's the way you feel. We Christophers never outstay our welcome. But I still fail to understand those pyjamas.'

'Where did you get that black eye?' asked Mr Bunting, ever anxious for information.

'Never you mind about my black eye. Who are you?'

'I am Lord Tilbury's solicitor.'

'Bunting,' thundered Lord Tilbury, 'show this young blot out. I'm going back to bed,' he said, and without more words hurried up the stairs at a speed quite creditable in a man of his build.

Biff followed him with a perplexed eye.

'What's he going to bed for?'

'I would be at as much a loss as yourself,' said Mr Bunting, 'had he not explained the situation to me. It appears that he invited an important business associate to lunch today and completely forgot the appointment. A Mr Llewellyn, a prominent Hollywood magnate, who is a touchy man and takes offence easily. Mr Llewellyn, I gather, spends a great many thousands of pounds a year advertising in Tilbury's papers, and Tilbury was afraid that if he found out the truth, he would withdraw his advertising. Fortunately Tilbury's secretary with great presence of mind told Mr Llewellyn that Tilbury had been taken ill and was in bed at his Wimbledon residence, and Mr Llewellyn said he would make a point of looking in in the course of the afternoon to see how he was. So Tilbury had no option but to go to bed.

I think this clears up the mystery of the pyjamas satisfactorily. If there are any points you wish touched upon, I shall be delighted to clarify them for you.'

It was not easy for Biff to stare with only one eye, but he managed to do so.

'You mean if this Llewellyn guy finds out that Tilbury stood him up, Tilbury'll lose a packet?'

'That is substantially the case.'

'Gosh!' said Biff, and he, too, headed for the stairs, followed at a slower and more senile pace by Mr Bunting, who was finding all this quite absorbing.

'Ah, Llewellyn,' said Lord Tilbury as the door opened, speaking in the same weak tone he had used before. Then, as he beheld Biff, his voice strengthened. 'I told you to get out!'

'And in due season,' said Biff, 'I will. But first there is a little business matter to be taken up. I think we can do a deal. I have here an agreement, drawn up by my solicitor, whereby ... Is it whereby, Bunting?'

'Quite correct.'

'Whereby you consent to waive all claim to the Pyke millions in return for a cut of five per cent of the gross.'

'You're insane!'

'I'm not so sure, Tilbury,' said Mr Bunting. 'It seems a generous enough settlement, and I would advocate its acceptance.'

'Sign here,' said Biff, 'on the dotted line.'

'I shall do nothing of the sort.'

'You will, if you don't want me to spill the facts to this Llewellyn guy when he arrives.'

Lord Tilbury gasped.

'This is blackmail! Can I have him arrested?'

'I never saw a chap with such a passion for arresting people,' said Mr Bunting amusedly. 'Such an action would certainly not lie. Blackmail involves the extortion of money, and so far from trying to extort money from you, this gentleman is offering to give you some.'

'Well spoken, Bunting.'

It was Biff who said this, not Lord Tilbury. The latter's

comment, if he had made one, would have been radically different.

'A bird in the hand is worth two in the bush, my dear Tilbury,' said Mr Bunting with the air of a man who has invented a happy phrase. 'These actions for setting wills aside are always chancy affairs, and from what you have told me your brother's fortune was quite large enough to make five per cent of it well worth having. I recommend the settlement.'

'Bunting, you are on the beam. A Daniel come to judgement.'

Again it was Biff who spoke, and again Lord Tilbury preserved a gloomy silence. His solicitor's words, so obviously spoken by a man who knew, had crushed the last remains of his spirit. He reached out a hand for the document, and Mr Bunting obligingly supplied the fountain pen without which he never stirred abroad.

There was something in the slow and painful way in which the head of the Mammoth Publishing Company signed his name that would have reminded Jerry Shoesmith, had he been present, of the Sergeant at the Paris police station. But eventually the sad task was completed. Mr Bunting added his signature as witness, and Biff with a cheery word of farewell withdrew.

3

'Nice young fellow,' said Mr Bunting, who had taken quite a fancy to him. 'I wonder how he got that black eye.'

'I wish I'd given it to him,' said Lord Tilbury morosely.

'He seems to have got married to your niece very suddenly. Had she said anything to you of her matrimonial plans?'

'No.'

'The thing came on you as a surprise?'

'Yes.'

'Ah well, in the Spring a young man's fancy lightly turns to thoughts of love, and this is no doubt true of young women also. Ah, the telephone,' said Mr Bunting. 'Excuse me.'

He was absent some minutes. When he returned, he had news.

'That was your friend Llewellyn. He says he is extremely sorry but he will be unable to be with you this afternoon. Something – he did not tell me what – has, as he expressed it, come up. He sends his kindest regards and hopes you will soon be in your usual robust health once more.'

Lord Tilbury quivered inside his yellow and purple pyjamas. The words had been a dagger in his heart. As he reflected that if only this fool of a motion picture magnate had had the sense to call up five minutes sooner, he would not have been compelled to sign that agreement, the iron entered into his soul.

'Must be a nice fellow,' said Mr Bunting, who was liking everyone this afternoon. 'Thoughtful. Considerate. Are you getting up?'

'Of course I'm getting up. No sense in lying in bed now.'

'True. Very true.'

Lord Tilbury climbed out of bed and put on his clothes. He was feeling low and depressed, and precisely as had been the case with Biff and Percy Pilbeam his thoughts had turned to that well-stocked cellar of his.

'I don't know what you're going to do, Bunting,' he said, 'but after I've telephoned my secretary to send the car I am going to have a drink.'

'I will join you if you have any non-alcoholic elderberry wine.'

'I haven't.'

Mr Bunting sighed.

'It's a curious thing that very few people have,' he said. 'I have often remarked it.'

With a cobweb-covered bottle and a glass in the drawing-room, Lord Tilbury began to feel a little better, but the restoration of his tissues was interrupted by the ringing of the telephone. Mr Bunting, ever courteous, went out into the hall to answer it. When he came back, his air was grave. He looked like a vulture whose mind is not at ease.

'Do you know who that was, Tilbury? That was the police.'

'The *police*?'

'Speaking from the local station. Do you by any chance know a man named Pilbeam? You do? Well, a rather unfortunate thing has happened. You recall the burglar I locked in the cellar?'

'Well?'

'It appears that that was Pilbeam, whoever Pilbeam may be. You apparently gave him your key, and he entered through the front door. I imagine he had come to see you about something, possibly some business matter, and nobody more surprised than he when he found himself arrested and taken off to the police station.'

'Serve him right.'

'Quite. But have you envisaged what will be the outcome?'

'I don't understand you.'

'Obviously he has grounds for an action for false arrest and imprisonment, and I cannot see how he can fail to mulct you in very substantial damages. I shall be much surprised if he is not on his way here now.'

4

Mr Bunting was perfectly correct. Percy Pilbeam was at that moment approaching The Oaks at the rate of knots, his soul, such as it was, seething like a cistern struck by a thunderbolt. On his previous visit he had not been in any too sunny a frame of mind, but his feelings then were merely tepid compared with his feelings now. He had had a testing time at the local police station, the tendency on the part of the Force having been to be sceptical as to his motives for being on what they called enclosed premises. The general disposition had been to classify him as a dangerous member of the underworld caught with the goods.

It was only when he had exhibited the front door key of The Oaks and the cheque signed Tilbury that his story of being a respectable friend of the family paying a social call had begun to receive credence. In the end he had been allowed to depart and had even been offered apologies, but this had done nothing to diminish his animosity and his resolve, as Mr Bunting had put it, to mulct Lord Tilbury in very substantial damages. Mentally phrasing it in a way which would never have met with the approval of Lionel Spenser, he proposed to soak Lord Tilbury good.

He was passing through the main gate with this purpose in mind, when he heard his name called and, turning, perceived an ornate car with an ornate chauffeur at the wheel and was aware of his cousin Gwendoline's lovely head protruding from a side window.

'Percy,' said Gwendoline, 'what on earth are you doing here?'

'Gwen,' said Percy, making the thing a duet, 'what on earth are you doing here?'

'Lord Tilbury rang for the car, and I thought I'd come along. He seemed all upset about something. His voice sounded so sad.'

'It'll sound sadder when I get hold of him,' said Percy grimly. 'He'll be lucky if he gets out of this for ten thousand pounds.'

'Why, whatever do you mean?'

In burning words Percy related the tale of the wrongs that had been done him, and Gwendoline's beautiful eyes widened as she listened.

'You mean you're going to sue him?'

'Am I going to sue him! You bet I'm going to sue him.'

'No, you aren't,' said Gwendoline, and there was a steely note in her voice. Her azure eyes, so soft when meeting those of her employer, were hard. 'You certainly aren't, and I'll tell you why. You start anything, young Perce, and I'll tell Biff what you told me about plotting his ruin with that Murphy friend of yours. And do you know what Biff'll do? He'll butter you over the pavement. You wouldn't want your block knocked off, would you, Perce? You wouldn't want to wake up in hospital with nurses smoothing your pillow and doctors asking you where you want the body sent?'

An erring husband, whom in the early days of the Argus

Agency he had trailed to a den of assignation, had once said much the same thing to Percy Pilbeam. He had not liked it then, and he did not like it now. He was not one of your Philip Marlow or Mike Hammer private investigators who enjoy violence and thrive on it, counting that day lost when they have not had the stuffing beaten out of them by cold-eyed men in Homburg hats. And he had seen enough of Biff to recognize that, though slight of build, he was exceedingly wiry and muscular, and it had always been foreign to his policy to encourage hostile thoughts in the minds of wiry, muscular men.

It did occur to him that if he allowed himself to be assaulted by Biff and could arrange for it to be done in the presence of witnesses, he could have him arrested and so increase the Pilbeam bank balance by two thousand pounds, but even at two thousand pounds he could not bring himself to feel that he would be making a good bargain. All his life he had had a strong distaste for being hit on the nose, and it was on the nose, something told him, that Biff would hit him first, before going on to other portions of his anatomy. The fire died out of his eye and his jaw dropped.

'You couldn't prove I told you that,' he said weakly.

'Oh, couldn't I? How could I have heard anything about it, if you hadn't told me? Biff'll believe it, anyway, which is all that matters. Did you know he was what they call an inter-collegiate boxing champion when he was at college over in America?'

A coldness came over Percy, starting at the feet.

'Oh, all right,' he said bitterly. 'Have it your own way.'

'Well, don't you forget,' said Gwendoline. 'Okay, Watson, drive on. Home, James, and don't spare the horses.'

5

The sight of Gwendoline Gibbs always had much the same effect on Lord Tilbury as did that of a rainbow in the sky on the poet Wordsworth, but he had never been gladder to see her than he was now, for seldom had he felt a greater need of being cheered up. No newspaper proprietor likes to be in the toils of a private investigator, and Mr Bunting had made it distressingly clear that Lord Tilbury was in those of Percy. Percy had a cast-iron case and there was practically no limit, said Mr Bunting with a sort of horrible relish, to the damages juries dealt out for wrongful arrest and imprisonment.

When, therefore, Gwendoline revealed that she had met Percy and reasoned with him and persuaded him to drop the suit, such a surge of love and gratitude filled the proprietor of the Mammoth Publishing Company that only the thought of Mr Pilbeam senior kept him from proposing on the spot.

'You are invaluable, Miss Gibbs,' he cried. 'I don't know what I should do without you.'

Gwendoline broke the bad news.

'I'm afraid you're going to have to do without me, Lord Tilbury. Mr Llewellyn wants to take me back to Hollywood with him. He said he had never seen anyone so photogenic.'

Lord Tilbury's heart stood still. It then throbbed like a dynamo, and a moment later he was laying it at her feet. The thought that if he did not speak now, this girl would be lost to him for ever overcame his misgivings about Mr Pilbeam senior. To win her he was prepared to call Mr Pilbeam Uncle Willie with every sentence he uttered.

'Don't do it!' he cried. 'Don't dream of going to Hollywood!'

'But I'm photogenic. Mr Llewellyn says so. He says I have a great future in pix.'

'Damn Mr Llewellyn and damn pix! Stay here and be my wife!'

'Oh, Lord Tilbury!'

'Don't call me Lord Tilbury. Call me George.'

Gwendoline giggled. 'It sounds so funny.'

'What sounds funny?'

'Calling you George.'

'I see nothing funny in it at all.'

'Nothing funny in what?' asked Mr Bunting, appearing from nowhere.

Lord Tilbury regarded him sourly.

'Bunting!'

'Yes, Tilbury?'

'Go for a walk!'

'But I've just been for a walk.'

'Go for another.'

'Why?'

'Can't you see I want to kiss her?'

Mr Bunting looked doubtful.

'It is not a thing I should advise on a full stomach.'

'Bunting!'

'It has been known to lead to apoplexy. There is a danger of embolism, brought about by a clot or other foreign body which is carried to the brain by the blood stream. I can assure you –'

'Bunting!'

'Yes, my dear fellow?'

'Do you want to be torn limb from limb?'

'Certainly not,' said Mr Bunting, who could imagine nothing less hygienic.

'Then go into the garden and stay in the garden and don't come out of the garden till you're told to.'

'Certainly, certainly, certainly.'

'Oh, Georgie,' said the future Lady Tilbury lovingly, 'you're so masterful.'

6

The uplifted feeling induced by the bulge in his pocket, where the signed agreement lay, had begun to ebb in Biff as he made his way through the grounds of The Oaks, Wimbledon Common. Recollection of last night's happenings was returning to him, and he could not rid himself of the conviction that among those happenings had been a fight, a brawl, a physical encounter between himself and a member of London's police force. It was all still very hazy, but definite enough to cast a shadow on what should have been a moment for joy and self-congratulation.

He had certainly become embroiled with someone last night – his injured eye testified to that – and more and more the impression began to solidify that this someone had worn a helmet, a uniform and a ginger moustache. The afternoon was warm, but as he walked with bowed head, probing into the past, a chill began to pervade his system.

His meditations were interrupted by the tooting of a horn, and looking up he saw Jerry at the wheel of a natty sports model car whose appearance was vaguely familiar. He stared at him haughtily. After what had occurred he was not at all sure he was on speaking terms with Jerry. But he had now recognized the car as Linda's, and his curiosity as to what Jerry was doing in a car belonging to a girl he had never met was so great that he was compelled to utter. His opening words, oddly enough, were the same as those addressed by Percy Pilbeam to Gwendoline Gibbs and by Gwendoline Gibbs to Percy Pilbeam.

'What on earth are you doing here?' he cried.

'Your wife asked me to look you up,' said Jerry. 'Congratulations on that, by the way.'

'Thanks.'

'How does it feel being married?'

'Jerry o' man,' said Biff, unbending completely and letting bygones be bygones, 'it's the most extraordinary thing. You remember what I told you about how I should become a different man after I'd married Linda. Well, I'd looked on the reforming process as a gradual affair, if you know what I mean. I thought it would set in imperceptibly over the years and that the alterations would take place little by little as time went by, if you're still following me. But the change has been instantaneous, o' man, absolutely instantaneous. Do you know what happened just now?'

'I'm sorry, no. I'm a stranger in these parts.'

'I wanted a drink. I found the key of old Tilbury's cellar. I hovered on the threshold and there before me were bottles and bottles, each charged to the brim with the right stuff. But I remembered I'd promised Linda I'd swear off, and I turned on my heel and walked away, leaving them unopened. That's what marriage does to you. And the amazing thing is that instead of kicking myself for passing up the opportunity of a lifetime, I'm pleased, happy, delighted. But how did you come to meet Linda? That's what's puzzling me.'

'Oh, that happened quite simply. I was at the flat, thinking of this and that, when she blew in and asked me to come and remove you, because she had heard that Tilbury was on his way here. Did he show up?'

'Oh yes, he arrived.'

'And kicked you out?'

'He hinted that I would be better elsewhere. I suppose you've come to take me back to Halsey Chambers?'

'That was the idea. Oh, by the way, talking of Halsey Chambers, a policeman called there just as I was leaving. He wanted to know if a gentleman who looked like a dachshund lived there.'

'Holy smoke!'

'Yes, it startled me, I must admit.'

'You said, of course, that he didn't?'

'Why, no. I couldn't lie to the police.'

Biff clutched his forehead.

'This wants thinking out, Jerry o' man. I can't stay here, because old Tilbury's given me the bum's rush. I can't go back to the flat, because the cops'll be watching it. And if I stay in the open, I'll get pinched for vagrancy. So what's the answer?'

Jerry laughed, and when Biff told him with some asperity that there was nothing to laugh at assured him that he was mistaken.

'Listen, Biff,' he said, 'I'm getting a lot of fun out of this and speaking for myself I could go on for ever, but I suppose the humane thing is to tell you what the cop went on to say. I think you'll be interested. He asked me if I could get hold of you and bring you to the sickbed of the ginger-moustached officer who used to be on duty outside Halsey Court. He wants to thank his brave preserver.'

'What are you talking about?'

'It's a stirring story. The ginger-moustached one was on his beat last night when what they call a gang of youths closed in on him, and he was being roughly handled, as the expression is, when suddenly a splendid young fellow who looked like a dachshund came bounding into the fray and saved him.'

Biff stared.

'You're kidding.'

'No, that's what happened, and I think I can see how it came about. You saw the cop getting massacred by the gang of youths and it infuriated you so to think it wasn't you who was doing the massacring that you sailed in and laid them out.'

Biff's one unwounded eye roamed over the grounds of The Oaks, Wimbledon Common, and never to any visitor had their suburban charms seemed so pronounced. Even the house itself looked good to him.

'You mean the cops aren't after me?'

'Only to shake you by the hand.'

'They aren't going to pinch me?'

'They'll probably give you a medal. And do you know another thing that'll make your day? You're going to have me as a brother-in-law.'

'What!'

'Ask Kay if you're not.'

'Ah, well,' said Biff, having considered this, 'one can't expect life to be all jam. We all have our cross to bear.'

'Aren't you rejoicing at the thought of having me for a brother-in law?'

'Did you say brother-in-law?' asked Mr Bunting, manifesting himself apparently from thin air in that peculiar way of his. 'Are you, too, going to be married?'

'I am.'

'So, it appears, is everybody. It's a most extraordinary thing. I have just left Tilbury. He's getting married. Mr Christopher was married this morning. And now you say you ... I didn't catch the name?'

'My name is Shoesmith.'

'And now you, Mr Shoesmith, are about to be married. It's like some sort of epidemic. Are you gentlemen returning to town?'

'That's right.'

'Perhaps you will give me a lift?'

'Delighted.'

'And then, if you will allow me,' said Mr Bunting, 'I will take you to my club and you shall join me in a cup of cocoa. I do not often drink cocoa, as I find it hard to digest, but this is an occasion.'

The revellers got into the car and drove off, all eager for the treat. It was not long before Jerry began to sing, and after a while Biff and Mr Bunting joined him, Mr Bunting doing perhaps more than any of the trio to startle pedestrians and traffic. He had a pleasing and distinctive singing voice, not unlike that of a buzzard suffering from laryngitis. The dramatic critic of the *Petersfield Sentinel* would probably have described it as adequate.